The Learning of Paul O'Neill

The Learning of Paul O'Neill

Graeme Woolaston

Millivres Books
Brighton

First published in 1993 by Millivres Books (Publishers)
33 Bristol Gardens, Brighton BN2 5JR, East Sussex, England

ISBN 1 873741 12 X

A CIP catalogue record for this book
is available from the British Library

Typeset by Hailsham Typesetting Services, 4-5 Wentworth House,
George Street, Hailsham, East Sussex BN27 1AD

Printed and bound in Great Britain

Distributed in the United Kingdom and Western Europe by Turnaround
Distribution Co-Op Ltd, 27 Horsell Road, London N5 1XL

Distributed in the United States of America by InBook, 140 Commerce
Street, East Haven, Connecticut 06512USA

The author wishes to thank the Trustees of the National Library of
Scotland for permission to quote from 'Scotland' by William Soutar, from
Poems of William Soutar (Edinburgh, 1988), and Christopher Whyte for
permission to quote from 'Uírsgeul', from *Vírsgeul* (Gairm Books, 1991).

to

Peter Burton

The Learning of Paul O'Neill

Graeme Woolaston grew up in central Scotland and now lives near Glasgow, where he works as an arts administrator. In his spare time he listens to Mozart, drinks real beer, and rides a very small motor-bike (not simultaneously). He is the author of one previous novel, *Stranger Than Love* ('a gritty, sometimes frightening, always compelling novel', *Gay Times*, London; 'fascinating and incredible . . . a substantial and memorable book', *TWT*, Houston, Texas).

Author's Note

Although this book is set mostly in Scotland it doesn't assume that the reader is Scottish, and therefore Scots words and expressions, and references to distinctive Scottish practices, are explained where their meaning might not be apparent from the context. However the reader who is curious to know more will find short notes at the back. In particular, English readers who are puzzled by references to the very distinctive Scottish education system will find a brief outline of the ways in which it differs from the system they are familiar with.

On the other hand the book does tend to assume that the reader is gay or lesbian. It contains passages of sexual description which some non-gay readers may find offensive and disturbing.

Readers who know central Scotland may feel that they can identify the town on which 'Eassord' is based, and will perhaps find the use of some imaginary place-names to be an intrusion. Nonetheless these fictional place-names have two important functions. Firstly, they enable me to take outrageous liberties with actual topography when it suits my purpose, so that on several key occasions Paul sees vistas which in reality are either physically impossible or don't exist at all. Secondly, they help to emphasise that this book is fiction. I gave Paul the same start in life as myself, but then sent him in a radically different direction; moreover he is a Celt and not a Saxon; as a result his life is considerably more turbulent than my own has been – and also, I fear, considerably more interesting.

GW

Yet gifts should prove their use:
I own the Past profuse
Of power each side, perfection every turn:
Eyes, ears took in their dole,
Brain treasured up the whole:
Should not the heart beat once
'How good to live and learn'?

Robert Browning
'Rabbi Ben Ezra'

ONE

A SPRINGTIME OF BEGINNINGS

It is owre late for fear,
Owre early for disclaim,
Whan ye come hameless here
And ken ye are at hame.

William Soutar
'Scotland'

Paul enjoyed cycling dangerously on ice. From his home village, Chapelwell, to his school, Eassord Academy, he had to cycle about two miles along a country road which ran between fields on the southern edge of town. Then he turned into an unmade, rutted, pot-holed lane, along which something too small and untidy even to be called a hamlet straggled on either side. At the end of the lane were the bright brick-and-glass rectangular blocks of the Academy.

The lane was where the ice and the danger were, and on this frosty March morning Paul anticipated with pleasure the challenge of once again cycling the last half-mile to school as fast as he could, weaving from side to side to avoid the pot-holes, never touching his brakes, skirting the deep, ice-filled ruts with a skill which he owed to the fact that this was his Third Year at the Academy, the third winter he had negotiated this lane day after day.

Only fresh snow stopped Paul cycling. Otherwise, to have given up simply on account of the weather would have been sappy as far as he was concerned. New snow made cycling physically impossible, but as soon as the ploughs had cleared the main road, and the lane had had some rudimentary gritting, he was back on wheels again. He hated walking to school, as he hated cycling slowly.

Despite the frost Paul had no coat on; he was in a blue blazer, blue-and-white school scarf, and grey flannels. Lately he had begun to grow rapidly, and as a consequence had become even thinner than he had been as a child. He considered himself to be painfully skinny. His dark hair was still cut as a short back-and-sides; neither at home nor at school was he permitted to let it grow into the style the Beatles had made fashionable. It remained restless and uncontrollable. Every morning he Brylcreemed it, but usually the result was just to make it spiky, rather than well-groomed.

Paul was proud of his cycling skills, and put them to the test again this morning. At this hour, a quarter to nine, the lane was almost empty of pedestrians, and there were only a handful of other cyclists to worry about; this was the rear approach to the school. The majority of kids of his age in the village went to Eassord's junior secondary, which was on the other side of town. Only about a third of each year in Chapelwell Primary passed their eleven-plus, and went to the Academy.

Just once in three winters had Paul crashed on the ice, skidding across the lane on his shoulders, but without hurting either himself or the machine. This morning he maintained his record, and when he parked his bike in the sheds he was happy, with the elation produced by frost and exercise.

But as he turned towards the Boys' Entrance he was conscious of a shadow over the prospect of the morning. It was Tuesday: which meant swimming, after the mid-morning break. Swimming. Paul hated it: not so much the activity itself as what followed it, the whole business of the showers.

Then, abruptly, as he walked up the tarmac towards the door, his stomach tensed with fear. Tuesday. Swimming. Not Thursday. Not PE.

He couldn't stop here and look in his bag. He waited till he was indoors, amongst the muddle and ferocious noise of schoolboys (the girls had a separate entrance and cloakroom). He edged his way towards a wall, propped himself against it, and balancing his bag on one knee, opened it and looked inside. The inspection was unnecessary. He had known what he was going to find. Instead of a towel with his swimming-trunks wrapped inside, he saw gym-shoes and a pair of white PE shorts. When he had packed his bag the night before – an orderliness his mother had left to him – he had mixed up the days.

Quietly he closed his bag and looked around for his friends, as if unconcerned. But his fear, which had been vague and threatening, now was precise, sharply-focussed, and growing more intense by the moment. Oh bloody hell. Bloody shit, hell, hell, hell, *fuck*. He had brought the wrong kit with him. The penalty was unvarying and simple. He was in for three of the belt.

At break Paul usually bought two chocolate biscuits from the tuck-shop. Today, he wasn't exactly hungry.

He stood leaning on a parapet near the front of the school, looking over its playing fields towards the new houses on this side of the town, and beyond, about a mile away, the Castle Rock on which the Royal Burgh of Eassord had originally been built. The long, low buildings of the Castle stood at the height of the crag, which tailed eastwards with towers and a steeple, down into the modern town at its foot. Behind that, the high slopes of the Fetternmore Hills rose abruptly from the plain. There was snow on their peaks, which was unusual this close to spring. In other circumstances it would have been a beautiful, if cold, morning.

The same hills dominated the view of Eassord from Chapelwell, which was about two miles to the south of the town. When he had been in Primary Three Paul had sung the old Scots psalm:

> I to the hills will lift mine eyes
> From whence doth come mine aid . . .

And he had imagined, at seven, that God lived up there, amongst the summits of the Fetternmores. Well, he had been taught better since then; that there was no God in the hills or anywhere else, no aid from whence to come for anyone.

> The moon by night shall thee not smite,
> Nor yet the sun by day . . .

Perhaps not, but Maclaren's belt was going to. Paul's fear had grown till his stomach was now almost a numbness: as if he was too scared to be any longer scared. It wasn't just the thought of the pain the belt could cause; it was knowing that you weren't supposed to show, by the slightest wince, that you were being hurt.

Paul was certain he couldn't manage this. He was too soft. At primary school he had been strapped a few times, but never so that it really hurt. At the Academy things were different. He had been strapped twice here, and neither time had he been able to keep his face as impassive as he should have done, though he had avoided the absolute disgrace of actually flinching and drawing his hand away.

This would be only his third Academy belting. Then he remembered: almost exactly a year ago, to the very month, he should have been strapped again. The circumstances were very similar to today's. He'd forgotten his Latin books. Tully (his real name was Tulloch) had a 'policy' for this situation. If you were a girl, you got lines; if you were a boy, you were given the choice of lines or the belt. But in reality, as Tully and everyone else knew perfectly well, there was no choice. No boy could possibly, ever, opt for lines to avoid a belting. The consequences among the rest of the class would be intolerable; you would never be able to live down the reputation of being yellow, a total sap. Throughout the periods before Latin Paul had nerved himself, in the same state he was in now, to say what he would have to say: "the belt, please, sir".

But when, at the beginning of the Latin period, he had stood up and admitted he had no books with him, to his astonishment he saw a look of pure dismay cross Tully's face. There was a silence of several moments before, scarcely believing, he heard Tully say quietly:

"OK, O'Neill. Share with Elliott."

A murmur of surprise, perhaps even disapproval, ran round the class. It was a second or two before Paul could collect himself and pull his chair across the aisle to Mike Elliott's desk. Then, as he sat down, he understood why he had been let off. It was because it was barely a month since his mother died. And mixed with his relief, which was flooding him like an ending of pain in itself, there was bitter humiliation, and even anger at the teacher. He hated, he just could not stand, this reaction to what had happened to him. 'The poor, motherless boy'. It was unbearable.

The harsh electric bell rang on the school wall, making Paul jump. He turned to go in. Well, this was it now. There would be no getting out of it this time.

When Maclaren came into the changing-room – he was a short, greying man whom, normally, Paul rather liked – he said to Paul:

"Well, O'Neill, what's up with you?"

"I've forgotten my kit, sir."

Maclaren frowned.

"*All* of it?"

"I've brought my PE kit by mistake, sir."

Behind the teacher Paul saw several boys, in their trunks, turn to watch and listen.

"Have you got your gym shorts with you?"

"Yes sir."

"Well, get stripped then. And hurry up." He turned towards the class. "Right, you lot, form a line."

Good Christ, Paul thought. Have I got a guardian angel, or something? But as he hung his blazer on his peg a dismaying realisation struck him:

"Sir . . . "

"What now, O'Neill?"

"I haven't got a towel."

Maclaren frowned again.

"Well, you'll have to share with someone. Elliott – can you share your towel with O'Neill?"

A tall, blond boy, in blue trunks, answered:

"Yes, sir."

"Good. And get a move on, O'Neill, or the period'll be over before you've got your pants off."

Paul stripped quickly, following his usual procedure. He took off his shoes and socks, his trousers and his underpants, and hurriedly pulled up his shorts, before he even undid his tie. He hated, he totally and utterly hated, being naked in front of the other boys.

By the time he crossed to the entrance to the showers, which led through to the pool, he was the only boy left in the changing-room. At the showers he had to stop to let Maclaren examine his feet, for any sign of veruccas. As he balanced himself against the wall with one hand Maclaren said quietly:

"Right, O'Neill. When you go through, wait by the

poolside for me."

Instantly Paul's stomach lurched. So he wasn't getting off after all. Oh bloody, bloody fuck.

He stepped through the foul-smelling antiseptic dip and into the chill of the swimming pool, where the rest of the class were already in the water. He took up position, as he had been instructed, near the shallow end. Already he was consciously controlling his face muscles, making an effort to look unfrightened. He tried not to notice that several boys noticed he wasn't joining them, and suddenly, suspiciously, became keen on swimming up to the shallow end. One of them, his blond hair plastered down over his forehead, was Mike Elliott. Paul adjusted his shorts. They felt very uncomfortable; in the gym he would have had his underpants underneath, but right now everything inside was unsupported and loose. Maclaren came through the public door of the pool, on to the viewing platform, and down a short flight of steps to stand in front of Paul. His belt, folded double, was in his hand.

"Right," he shouted at the class, "form up over there" – and he pointed to the far side of the pool. Then he turned towards Paul, unfolding his belt, and simply looked at him. Paul didn't need to be told what to do. He held out both his hands, one resting on the other.

Maclaren leaned forward, put his left hand under Paul's crossed hands, and made him raise them to shoulder height. Paul's stomach tensed even tighter; he knew this was being done so that he would get the full force of each descending stroke. He looked up at the high windows of the pool, streaming with condensation, sparkling as the sun shone in. Everything seemed to have gone quiet.

In the open space of the pool the first stroke resounded much more loudly than it would have done in a classroom. Paul had no idea what the other two sounded like. After the first he was conscious only of the pain, blinding and repeated, and of his face: to keep his face still, keep it still. The belting took just seconds. Paul knew that if it hadn't been done quickly – but it always was – he could not have managed to keep his arms steady and his hands in place.

But he had done. He had!

"OK, O'Neill," Maclaren said.

Paul lowered his eyes from the window and let his arms drop. Maclaren was already folding the belt into the pocket of his track-suit.

"Get into place," he said.

Paul moved. He was longing, all but overwhelmingly, to rub his right hand, which he'd held uppermost, against his shorts, or press it against the cool rail by the pool steps, or plunge it into the water – anything which would make it hurt less. The pain even seemed to be intensifying, as if the strokes were burning themselves into his palm.

But he hadn't winced! And he wasn't going to show now that he was in pain; he could endure this for the few minutes it would last. He stood between two boys, and adjusted his shorts again. As he did so he surreptitiously let himself rub his palm once into his side. Then, briefly, he rubbed his hands together, as if he was cold. Already, he noted with surprise, the pain was starting to fade and give way to an unpleasant numbness, making his fingers feel as if they were swollen.

"Right," Maclaren said. "Half-a-dozen breadths."

Paul jumped into the pool and began the inelegant but effective style of swimming which was all he had ever been able to master.

It was several minutes before he came out of the water, by which time his hand was hurting only slightly, and he was able, after his concentrated efforts earlier, to let his face relax again. He sat by the pool edge, waiting for Maclaren's next instructions. His shorts seemed more uncomfortable than ever. He glanced down at them.

Immediately he felt himself starting to blush fiercely. To his horror the white cotton had become transparent: he was presented with – and was presenting to others – a blurred but perfectly discernible image of the dark mass of his pubic hair, and a clear view of his cock; even its pinkness showed through the cloth. He tugged at the shorts' waistband, pulling them up. His pubic hair became less visible, but at the price of making his cock more obvious than ever.

"Right," Maclaren ordered, "you lot" – it included Paul – "along to the deep end."

Reluctantly Paul stood up, and still more reluctantly began walking by the poolside.

For the remaining fifteen minutes of the lesson Paul moved and acted like an automaton, doing what he was told, but conscious, every time he was out of the water, of little except that everyone could see through his shorts. Again and again he tugged at them and tried to adjust them, but nothing would make them stop clinging to his cock. From behind he imagined he might as well be naked. Several boys grinned at him, some as if they thought it was all a joke, others taking obvious pleasure in his embarrassment. One boy, when Maclaren was turned away, dropped his hand to his waist, wiggled his forefinger obscenely, and laughed. Paul felt as if his cock was about a foot long; if it was possible to do such a thing, he believed he was blushing non-stop. This was hell.

He usually dreaded the end of the swimming period more than any other part of it, but today he was glad to join the line-up for the showers, and still more glad that Maclaren didn't repeat the command he had given a number of times in recent weeks: "Right, you lot, get your pants off in the showers." Under the hot water, the one wholly pleasurable sensation of the period, Paul saw that he wasn't alone in refusing to strip. At the beginning of their Third Year, of the fifteen boys in the class only a minority had showered naked; now, thanks to Maclaren's pressure, the balance had tipped the other way, but about half-a-dozen boys still kept their trunks on.

Paul not only loathed the idea of being seen naked himself, he didn't like it when other boys were naked either. He was certain they looked better – well, that was, some of them did, those who had well-made bodies – that they looked better in their trunks, or in PE shorts, or, in the changing-room, in their white Y-fronts. In fact, he could enjoy seeing boys like that: especially if their shorts, like his own, really were short, and not, like some people's, baggy and flapping about. Or in smooth swimming trunks, of shining nylon. Stripped, but still decent; not showing you all their ugly bits and making you blush.

As he showered he tried not to listen to what was being said around him, in case some of it referred to himself. And sure enough, that fatso Robinson, whose bent dick made him even uglier in the nuddy than the rest, cried out:

"Hey, Neilly, why haven't you got your shorts off? We've all seen your works today."

Paul ignored him, but he persisted: "Come on, Neilly, you've no secrets from us now."

There was general laughter, which grew when Paul, bright red, answered just: "Sod off, Robbo."

In the changing-room he stood beside Mike Elliott, waiting to use his towel. Mike was naked. He was one of those who had always stripped in the showers, and he had let it be known that he couldn't understand why anyone else should make a fuss about doing so. But Paul liked him. In school they had a casual but acknowledged friendship; they called each other by their christian names, and not by nicknames – something which, as far as Paul could remember, Mike had started. Yet they hardly ever met outside school, and Paul had never been to Mike's house. Now, standing watching him dry himself, Paul briefly envied him. He had a nice body, even in the nude, and he wasn't in the least ashamed of any part of it. Perhaps he was right, after all; perhaps that was the only sensible attitude.

"Why don't you take your shorts off, Paul?"

"Don't *you* start, I've just had Robbo having a go at me."

Mike dried his shoulders and grinned.

"You're not getting this towel till you take your shorts off."

"Oh, come on Mike, don't mess about."

Mike rubbed the towel across his torso and grinned still more widely: "No. No towel till you take your shorts off."

"Look, Mike, get a move on, will you? Or I'll be late for the next period."

"Then you'll just get the belt again, won't you?"

With a jolt Paul realised he had completely forgotten

about his strapping. He glanced down at his right hand and then exclaimed: "Good God!"

"What's up?"

Paul answered by holding out his hand for Mike to see. On his palm there were bluish outlines of the belt's two tails.

"Hey," Mike said, and turned round to the others. "Look at Neilly's hand." A couple of boys took up the invitation, but said nothing.

"I didn't think I'd got it so hard," Paul said. He was about to ask Mike if *his* hand marked like that when he was belted; but Mike interrupted him by handing him his towel: "There you are, then."

"Thanks."

Paul dressed in the reverse order to that in which he'd undressed. He put on his shirt and pullover before he tugged down his shorts, dried himself round the middle as quickly as he could, and pulled up his underpants with the relief he always felt at this point in the swimming period: that was that over again, for another week.

Paul cycled home more carefully than he had done in the morning; he felt he'd had enough pain for one day. Even though it was still daylight the lane and even the road were icing up again.

The core of Chapelwell was an old-fashioned Scottish village, stretched along a single street from the school and the church. But about twenty years before, after the War, the hillside on which the village was built had been cleared back of trees to make way for a large, roughly circular scheme of council houses. This was where Paul lived, about half-way up the hill. It took all the strength of his legs to cycle the last couple of hundred yards, but today, as usual, he managed it. He parked and chained his bike at the back of the house before going round to the front to let himself in.

For the next hour, till his father got home from work at half-past-five, he would have the house to himself. His first action was to go the tape-recorder beside the television in the living-room, run off the tape which was on it – one of his father's – and replace it with one of his own which had a collection of songs recorded off 'Saturday Club' on the radio: Manfred Mann, the Kinks, Cilla Black, Herman's Hermits, and his favourites, the Beatles. At once the room was filled with music. He turned up the volume and went upstairs to change.

The room across the landing from his was empty. Till six months ago it had been Tom's, and it still was whenever he chose to come home from university, which wasn't often. As he pulled on his jeans Paul wondered how much he might have been able to tell Tom of today's events, if he were here. That he'd got the belt? Yes, almost certainly. That he'd nearly died of embarrassment all through the swimming period? Probably not. The truth was, though Paul was ashamed to admit it to himself, he wasn't sure he liked his own brother. The four years between them seemed to be an immense gap, and what made it worse was that there was something cold, perhaps even forbidding, about Tom. There were so many things he would have liked to ask his brother about, but which he couldn't. About a year ago he'd tried to tell Tom he'd had a wet dream, because he was startled by it, but Tom had brushed him off almost at once:

"That's just your age. We all get those at your age."

"Did you?"

"Oh, shut up, Paul."

And that was that. Though Paul knew he could never, ever, have mentioned to Tom what it was that most worried him about the few wet dreams he'd had. In every case, he'd woken up from dreaming about a boy – the very first time, that he was watching Mike take off his trunks in the showers, with fantastic excitement. The strangest aspect of this was that in real life he had never felt any such thing. But were dreams like this normal? Were they supposed to happen 'at your age'? Paul had no-one he could ask; and gradually he had come to assume they must be, that it was just part of everything else he didn't really understand – like growing pubic hair, and having your voice break. Everything in his life seemed to be changing and going on changing, and no doubt in due time his dreams would change as well, into dreams of girls.

He sat down on his bed – which was unmade, something his mother would never have tolerated – and looked at his right hand. The marks of his belting were faint, but obvious to himself. He pressed the balls of his palm. They hurt slightly, as if they were bruised beneath the skin. He repeated the sensation, and again, and again. Suddenly a thrill of pride went through him: he was tougher than he'd thought, another time he wouldn't be so frightened of the strap. His thrill repeated itself. He was getting to be more like other boys, more like Mike, who could take it without twitching a muscle.

At that moment the tape downstairs began playing 'I Wanna Hold Your Hand', the Beatles song which had been a hit the Christmas before last. Paul listened for a few moments and then joined in, but changing the words: "I wanna *hit* your hand – I wanna *hit* your hand . . . ". He threw back his head and roared with laughter. Then, as suddenly as his amusement had started, it went. The associations of the song had returned in one massive wave of memory which for several moments made him catch his breath.

The Christmas before last. His mother had been ill, too ill to eat more than a few mouthfuls of the Christmas dinner she'd insisted on preparing as usual, by herself. Just a stomach pain, just a sickness, she told them. She refused any fuss, even laughing at their attempts to help her: "Men in the kitchen," she'd said, "are about as much use . . .". In the first week of January she went into hospital. It was cancer of the liver. She was dying, at forty-two.

Paul's fourteenth birthday fell a fortnight later. In the infirmary, lying looking white and ghastly, but still smiling, she had a parcel for him. It was a new grey slipover for school. He had never worn it, not wanting it ever to get dirty or spoiled. She died in the second week of February.

Paul stood up and drew the curtains, leaned against the wall, and realised that yet again there were tears in his eyes. This room was the only place where he had ever cried for her. He supposed that across the landing Tom must have cried in *his* room, but that was yet something else they never talked about, were never able to talk about.

His parents' friends, and his grandparents, had nearly driven him demented in the weeks which followed his mother's death. Over and over again he was told how 'brave' he was being. "Paul has been very brave about it all." "Paul, you are a very brave young man." "Paul, you don't know how good it is that you've been able to be so brave and such a support to your father and your brother." (Couldn't Tom be a support to himself?) The adjective had become the most hated in the language for him. It was as if they really thought his grief – perhaps the illusion comforted them – was only moderate. But that was a double insult, both to himself and to his mother.

Paul wiped his eyes, crossed the room, and went back downstairs. He wanted to get some French homework done before tea. But as he took out his books and sat down at the living-room table, a question occurred to him. He didn't want to be brave, but he wanted to be tough. Did that make sense? Or was he crazy? If you thought about it, it seemed like a complete contradiction.

The tape had wound on and now was playing the song by that group with the girl drummer. Paul opened his French grammar and wondered, not for the first time, why the French had to have a past tense which they never actually spoke. Couldn't they have made do with two?

At swimming the next week Paul had his red trunks. As a result he enjoyed the period considerably more than the previous one, till at the end, when they were lining up to go into the showers, Maclaren came out with that command he seemed determined to force on them:

"Right, you boys. Trunks off in the showers, and get a move on about it. And that includes you, Parker. On you go."

In the showers everyone was quieter than usual. Paul glanced round. Parker hadn't done what he was told;

neither had three or four others. Paul's hands had been at the waist of his trunks. He took them away.

But as he stepped through into the changing-room, to his surprise he saw Maclaren standing there, which was unusual. Paul started to go past him; and at once heard Maclaren barking almost in his ear: "Get your pants off, boy!"

Paul kept going. His heart started to thump. At any moment he expected he would be called back, made to strip, and be sent into the showers again. This was it, now; he couldn't refuse a direct instruction from a teacher.

But nothing happened. Paul grabbed his towel, started to dry himself, and glanced round nervously. Maclaren was looking at him. Slowly, as if exasperated, he shook his head. Then, without saying anything more, he crossed the room and went out.

"You might as well give up, Paul."

Paul jumped: it was Mike, who had come up beside him without his having heard. He was grinning.

"Honestly, Paul, you're going to have to."

Paul was irritated: "Yeah, maybe."

Mike rubbed his towel across his chest: "Listen, Paul – how would you like to come round to my place for tea some evening? In fact, how about tonight?"

Paul was so taken by surprise he stopped drying himself. Mike said: "Is that OK?"

"Yeah – yeah, of course, thanks . . . Thanks!" He bent to dry his legs, and then straightened up again: "The only thing is – I'll have to let my Dad know . . ."

"Can you ring him at work?"

"Yes."

"Well, ring him from my place, then." Mike grinned again. "Is that fixed?"

"Yeah. Yeah, great!"

So that afternoon, at four o'clock, Paul cycled out of the front of the school rather than the back, into Eassord, with Mike beside him. It took them only minutes to reach Mike's place, which turned out to be a large, semi-detached house near the Royal Park, below the Castle Rock. As they put their bikes away in a garden shed at the back Paul realised he was surprised to find himself in this part of town, where the houses were considerably more posh than any in Chapelwell. Somehow he'd always imagined Mike lived in a council house, like himself.

When they went inside Mike asked, a little stiffly: "Fancy a coffee – or something like that?"

Paul couldn't stop himself smiling.

"I *can* make a cup of coffee," Mike said. "In fact, at last year's BB camp I was a cook."

"I thought they all looked a bit sickly when they got home."

"Do you want this coffee in your stomach or over your head?"

In the kitchen Mike explained: "The folks don't get back till about a quarter-to-six, so we can do what we like till then." Paul knew Mike was an only child. "Do you play snooker?"

"Never played it in my life."

"Good, I'll teach you."

Paul was astonished: "Have you got a snooker-table?"

"Well, we're not going to play it on the fucking floor, are we?"

Paul blushed at his stupidity.

After he had rung his father to tell him where he was they went upstairs to Mike's bedroom. It was about twice the size of his own. Airfix model aeroplanes hung on threads from the ceiling, there were posters of ships and planes all over the walls, and more Airfix models were on shelves and on the sideboard.

"I didn't know you went in for all this," Paul exclaimed, genuinely interested. He examined the models more closely; some of them, of houses and of a signal-box, he recognised: "Have you got a train set?" he asked.

"Well, I *used* to have." Paul glanced up and saw that Mike was embarrassed: "That's where those came from, of course."

They discussed the models, sipping from their mugs of

coffee; then Paul sat down on Mike's bed while Mike changed out of his uniform. To Paul's surprise he stripped right down to his underpants before, bending over, he began rummaging in a drawer. Watching him, Paul thought yet again how nice a boy could look when he was wearing just his Y-fronts; it was a pity Mike couldn't stay like that. Instantly he was horrified. What kind of way was that to think about a boy? What on earth would Mike say if he could imagine – which, thank God, he couldn't – that Paul was enjoying seeing him undressed? Mike straightened up with a tee-shirt in his hands, pulled it on, and turned to Paul as if he were about to speak; instead he frowned slightly. Paul looked down at the carpet, blushing deeply.

"Aren't you going to take off your blazer?" Mike asked.

Paul jumped up, glad of the distraction: "Yeah, sure."

Once Mike was fully dressed he led Paul across to another large room, in which there was a half-size snooker table.

"Fantastic!" Paul exclaimed.

Mike arranged the balls on the table and started giving Paul a summary of the rules of the game. After a while Paul interrupted him: "I know what to do, it's just that I've never done it."

Mike looked up. Suddenly he grinned widely.

"I should hope not, at your age."

It was a few moments before Paul understood. When he did, his reaction made Mike burst out laughing and exclaim: "Christ, you don't half blush easily, O'Neill! I've never known anyone to blush like you. You're *always* blushing about something."

"Oh, give over, Mike."

"But you are!"

Paul could see the joke against himself, but at the same time he was annoyed: "You don't have to tell me."

"You were even blushing because I was in my underpants! Weren't you?"

Briefly Paul was frightened. But in Mike's eyes he saw that Mike really did have no idea what he had been feeling: "I wasn't," he lied.

"Yes, you were. I bet I can make you blush just by saying, 'Paul, you're blushing'." Again he burst out laughing: "There you are! I told you so."

Even in his embarrassment Paul couldn't stop himself from laughing too: "Oh, shut up, and let's play this - ". He checked himself.

"'This fucking game', you were going to say. Eh?"

"No, I wasn't."

"Go on, say it."

"*Play*!" Paul ordered.

Inevitably, Mike won the first game easily, but before the end Paul was getting the hang of snooker; and at one point in their second game he was actually ahead.

"Are you *sure* you've never played this before?" Mike asked as Paul lined up on the green.

"Never. Oh, *yes!*" – as the ball went in.

"Bloody hell," Mike complained as he replaced the ball. Then, as Paul was trying to decide which red to go for next, he said: "Paul, do you mind if I ask you something?"

Paul didn't want the distraction: "What?"

"Why do you go to the Academy?"

The question was so unexpected Paul stood up, his cue in his hand.

"What on earth do you mean?"

"I mean – why don't you go to St Mungo's?"

Paul was mystified. Then, abruptly, he understood; he started to laugh: "Because I'm not a Catholic! Why – did you think I was?"

For once Mike was the more uneasy of them.

"Well, I didn't know . . . I mean – 'O'Neill', and all that." He grew more confident: "And you're a Celtic supporter, for fuck's sake! You're the only Celtic supporter I know."

Paul smiled.

"What would I be doing at a Protestant school, if I was a Catholic?"

"Well, that's what I didn't understand. I thought, maybe your parents – I mean . . .". He looked down at the floor, his face suddenly full of distress.

"My mother was a Protestant," Paul said quietly. "My

The Learning of Paul O'Neill

The Learning of Paul O'Neill

father *used* to be a Catholic. He gave it up when he married my mother."

"Oh, I see."

Paul bent over the table again: "They were married in 1943. My father says he had more important things to worry about at the time."

"But wasn't there a stooshie about it?"

Paul straightened up: "Oh yes, certainly. I don't think . . ." He tailed off. "My grandmother – that is, my father's mother – didn't go to my mother's funeral."

"Jesus!"

Paul felt he ought to defend the O'Neills: "But most of my father's family came. Apparently, though, it's against their religion. They're not supposed to go to Protestant funerals. Or weddings."

After a moment Mike said: "What a load of shit!"

Paul nodded slowly.

"Absolutely."

He bent down over the table again.

"So *you're* a Protestant, then?"

"Certainly not. I'm an atheist."

"Why do you support Celtic?"

Paul laughed.

"With half my family being Catholics? How could I support Rangers? They wouldn't even let me into Ibrox. My grandparents come from Donegal, you know."

"So you're half-Irish?"

"No, I'm pure Scots. My father was born in Glasgow, my mother in Eassord. Now, can I get on with this game?"

Several shots later, by which time he was in the lead, Mike said: "Paul – do you mind if I ask you something else?"

Paul looked up from the table, smiling.

"Is this a plot to put me off?"

Mike grinned.

"I was just wondering – why won't you take your trunks off after swimming?"

Paul stared up at him.

"What has *that* got to do with anything?"

"Well, it's just . . . people were impressed last week, you know. With the way you took it off Maclaren. He can really draw the belt."

Paul stood up: "Yes, I know." Once again he blushed; this time, he thought, more with pride than with embarrassment.

"But then," Mike went on, "you kind of threw it away again by being such a sap in the showers."

Paul, annoyed, went back to the game.

"What's sappy about it? And anyway, I'm not the only one."

"No, and you're all saps."

Paul knew that his blush was beginning to deepen into a distressing red. He took his shot, missed, and straightened up. Mike couldn't fail to see the effect that the turn in the conversation had produced in him, and yet, as he potted a ball, he carried on: "We all know what you've got, Paul. We're all made the same way."

Paul realised he was beginning to grow angry: "That's not the point."

Mike looked up.

"Of course it's the point. If that's not the point, what *is* the point?"

Paul searched hurriedly for an answer. He knew there had to be one, but he couldn't think of it; frustrated, he exclaimed: "Oh, give it a rest, Mike."

Mike potted the black, replaced it, and missed with his next shot.

"Your turn," he said. But as Paul was bending over he went on: "You know what you should do now, don't you?"

"What?"

"As well as stop being daft in the showers, I mean. Get yourself another belting."

"*What*?"

"You heard."

Paul, astounded, stood up.

"Have you gone completely loopy?"

Mike started to laugh: "Well, it would let people see for certain that you're not soft. That's what I did, in First Year."

"Did what?"

"Got myself the belt, of course. It's easily done. Me and Hutchie, we had a competition in second term to see which of us would get most strokes in the term. I won."

Paul stared at him. After a moment he started to smile.

"Yes, I think I remember now. We used to have" – he stopped, hesitated, and then felt that honesty compelled him to change what he'd been about to say: "There used to be belting leagues like that at our primary school. But I still say you're loopy."

"No, I wasn't. That way, I didn't have to get into any fights to prove myself. I can't fight for toffee. Saved me a lot of bother, that did."

Paul bent down and lined up for his shot. As he did so Mike asked: "How did *you* do in the league?"

Paul remained still, hoping he wasn't blushing yet again.

"I wasn't in it." The admission hurt. It was, he knew, a confession of weakness.

"Yeah," Mike said casually. "But just make an effort now, and you'll be in with the in-crowd."

"I think I'd rather be out with the out-crowd."

Mike said softly: "No, you wouldn't."

Paul completely miscued. As Mike took his place at the table he said: "Well, at least do what I told you in the showers." He lowered his head. "But I'll make a man of you one day."

"Maybe you should worry about making a man of yourself."

Mike's burst of laughter sent his cue rocketing wide of the cue-ball: "You cheeky bastard!" he exclaimed.

They had two more games of snooker; Mike won them all, though by decreasing margins. Over tea Paul met Mike's parents. The visit, he decided as he cycled home on another frosty night, had been great fun; apart from that one, annoying conversation.

But in bed he found his thoughts returning to it again and again. He knew Mike was right. No doubt about it, he was right.

He couldn't get to sleep. Eventually he resorted to a

device which he increasingly used in this situation; he began to work out the next stage in a story he was writing, in an old school jotter. Ever since he'd been eight or nine Paul had wanted to be a writer one day, with his name on the front of a book. He had only once ever told this to anyone; the laughter with which the idea was greeted had ensured he never made the admission again. No-one but himself knew about the jotters in which he scribbled his stories – usually, only to throw them away in disgust a week or two later. His present story was set on a different planet, and had three characters, all space travellers. He'd got the idea from *Dr Who*, which he never missed; he'd even made his Dad change the time of Saturday tea so that he could see it. In his jotter the characters were currently trapped in a cave by a huge, spider-like creature. Trying to work out how on earth he could rescue them, Paul drifted away into sleep.

All through the following week, at the most inconvenient moments, Mike would whisper to him: "You're blushing, Paul", not only making Paul duly blush but giving him a fit of the giggles, and then, usually, making himself laugh as well in reaction. When he did this in a French class they were spotted, and for a few moments Paul thought he was about to get the second belting Mike had suggested he try for. Instead, they were both given a hundred lines.

"You ought to do mine as well," Paul complained afterwards.

"Yes, I'm sorry," Mike said.

Paul hadn't expected this. Surprised, he laughed: "Oh, it doesn't matter."

In the evening he noted that the time it took to do a hundred lines was considerably longer than the time the pain of his strapping had lasted. Perhaps, he thought as he laboured on, bored and irritated, opting for the belt when you were given the choice wasn't just the necessary thing to do; it was positively sensible.

The following Tuesday he joined the line-up at the end of swimming feeling almost as nervous as he had done a fortnight earlier when he had been going the other way. He knew that if he hesitated he wouldn't manage to do what he intended; so as soon as he was amongst the jets of water he put his hands on his trunks, tugged them down, and chucked them on to the heap of wet trunks at the end of the showers.

He could only hope that his blushing – he'd abandoned in advance any idea that he might get through this without once again being plagued by his weakness – would look like the effect of the water, which after the chill of the badly-heated pool was almost painfully hot. Then he waited for the wisecracks and the ribbing.

Nothing happened. No-one seemed to notice that for the first time he had switched from the shy minority to the naked majority. It was only when he was by his clothes, drying himself quickly, that he got some reaction; as Mike came up beside him he grinned and winked.

"Go on," Paul said. "Say it again."

"Don't worry about it, kid."

"*Kid*?" Paul rubbed his towel across his shoulders, hesitated, and then spoke more quietly: "I'd have thought it was obvious now that I'm not a kid." It was the nearest he had come in his life to cracking a dirty joke; and he was delighted when Mike hooted with laughter.

The next Tuesday, Paul was more interested in what was going on in the outside world. It was the day of the first Gemini space flight, the first time America had launched a two-man capsule. Just five days earlier the Russian cosmonaut Leonov had become the first man to walk in space. Paul had followed the development of space flight avidly since the day, when he was in Primary Six, that Gagarin had orbited the earth. This Tuesday he was wishing he could be at home; the new communications satellites meant that pictures of the launch, if it went ahead on schedule, might be on tv .

Because his thoughts were elsewhere he stripped in the

showers less self-consciously than he had done the week before, though yet again, he realised with annoyance at himself, he blushed as his trunks came off. A moment later he was blushing a great deal more when a loud wolf-whistle resounded over the hissing of the shower-jets.

"Hey, get this! Neilly's showing his all!"

It was that bastard Robbo again. Paul ignored him. Robinson wolf-whistled again and started singing: "Come on, Neilly, show us your bum, show us your bum, show us your bum . . . "

Paul spun round: "I'm showing it, you fool."

There was an explosion of laughter under the showers. Instantly Robinson fell quiet. Paul, slightly dazed, realised he'd won the encounter.

But now Macintosh, a short, dark-haired, greasy boy whom Paul disliked, called out: "Hey, Neilly, how about swimming two lengths of the pool?"

"No way," Paul said at once.

But several other boys joined in: "Come on, Neilly, two lengths. Swim two lengths. Come on!"

Paul was silent. It wasn't uncommon for boys to do this when they were naked, but it was very risky, since at any moment a girl might walk in, or one of the women PE teachers. Just a few weeks before two boys from 3F had been caught at it, by a male teacher, and been given six of the belt each.

The clamour went on. Paul repeated: "No way."

Then Robinson found his voice again: "Dare you, Neilly. I dare you to do it."

Paul's stomach tensed. A dare was a serious matter.

"To the deep end and back, Neilly. Come on, it doesn't take thirty seconds."

Paul turned round: "Why don't you do it, then?"

He thought this would shut Robbo up again. But instead the boy pushed past him: "OK, I will. "

He disappeared out of the entrance to the pool. A second later there was a splash. Several boys crowded to the entrance, as close as they could, to watch; they cheered when Robinson returned, as he had said, hardly half a minute later.

"There you are," he said. "Nothing to it."

Paul stood beneath his shower, full of misery. He wished he had the courage to take up Robinson's dare, he knew that if he didn't . . . But he couldn't. He just couldn't.

He was only slightly consoled when Mike said to him, in the changing-room: "Don't worry about it, Paul. Robbo's a total arsehole. Ignore him."

But throughout the rest of the day the memory of the incident wouldn't leave him. He'd shown himself up again for what he really was – a coward.

No-one else, however, not even Robinson, referred to the matter again, and the following week he was left to shower in peace. Three days later the school broke up for the Easter holidays.

On the first Monday evening of the holiday, as they were preparing tea, his father said to him: "Paul, I'm going to be away all day on Wednesday."

There was something in his father's tone, a note of worry, which made Paul look round – he was laying the table: "Why?"

"I'm going up to Aberdeen for the day. I'm not taking the car, I'll just go by train. So I won't be back till about ten."

Paul was astonished. Aberdeen was where Tom was a student, but he was off on a geology vacation field trip.

"Is something wrong?"

"No, no" – his father looked round from the cooker – "no, it's just to do with work."

"Oh, I see." His father worked for an insurance firm.

"I'm going to spend a day at the Aberdeen office. Which means you'll be on your own till quite late. I thought, maybe you'd like to invite a friend round, or something?"

"Yeah – great!" He knew instantly who it would be. "I'll give Mike a ring." He felt like dashing to the phone there and then; but contained himself till after they had eaten.

Mike had a better idea: "Why don't we go off somewhere on our bikes together? Make a day of it?"

"Great!"

Which was what they did. Winter had ended abruptly the week before the holidays and given way to an exceptionally warm spring; it was like a bright morning in early summer when Mike called at Paul's house to collect him. By agreement, Mike was carrying sandwiches in his saddle-bag and Paul a bottle of orangeade. They cycled out of Chapelwell along an old country road which twisted below the Fells, the hills to the south of the village, till it joined the main road west out of Eassord. They were now on the flat agricultural plain of the Carse of Menteith. It was perfect terrain for cycling; the road headed straight towards the Grampian mountains, which formed the whole horizon in front of them.

After about a dozen miles they stopped for a drink. The unseasonal heat had made them so thirsty they had to buy a second bottle at a village shop before they turned northwards, crossing the Carse between fields which were green with the shoots of the new crops. They stopped for lunch at the Lake of Menteith. In the summer the area would be crowded with tourists, but today, in the first week of April, they had no problem finding a place to eat beside the lake, looking across its quiet ripples towards the peaks of Ben Lomond and Ben Venue. The sun, to their left, was high in the sky, and strong.

When they had eaten and drunk Mike said: "Right – I'm getting in some sunbathing."

He tugged off his pullover and his shirt in one go.

"You're mad," Paul said.

"No, I'm not – come on, you too."

"And I must be mad as well," Paul added as he complied. But Mike was right; as soon as he was stripped he could feel the warmth on his chest.

They leaned back on the grass, their shoes only inches from the lapping water. Behind them a copse of trees, through which they'd pushed their bikes, sheltered them from a slight easterly breeze and from the road they'd cycled along; but there were so few cars about today the spot hardly needed protection in that way.

Gradually Paul became aware that he was extraordinarily happy. All the colours in front of him seemed more intense than any colours he had ever seen before: the blue of the sky and the lake, the brown of the lower slopes, the deep, dark blue of the mountains below their lingering caps of snow. There seemed to be no sound but birdsong, filling the clearing where they lay.

After a long silence between them he said: "When I grow up, I'm going to come and live out here."

Mike turned to him. "Whatever for?"

"Because it's so peaceful."

"You'll get bored."

"No, I won't. I'll have a car. I'll be able to get into town whenever I want."

Mike turned away and smiled. "You're maybe right. Tell you what – I'll come and be your neighbour."

"I said I wanted to come here for *peace*. Ouch!" – this as Mike swiped him on his upper arm. He was grinning: "You're becoming a right cheeky bastard."

As he rubbed himself and laughed Paul felt a strange thrill go through him. The 'insult' summed up exactly what he would like to be – what, perhaps, he really *was* 'becoming'? Was that why Mike had lately, suddenly, seemed to want to be a much closer friend to him than he had been before?

By the time they left to cycle home the breeze had strengthened, and it was now in their faces. They headed eastwards across the Carse, seeing the Castle Rock of Eassord gradually grow larger and larger in front of them, dominating the gap between the Fetternmore Hills and the Fells. Tired, they stopped again to eat ice-creams in a village café. By the time they reached Eassord they were cycling only with difficulty. It had been Paul's plan to invite Mike to his house for the evening, but Mike insisted Paul have tea again at his place: "I'm far too knackered to ride out to Chapelwell again!"

Throughout the evening they talked, and laughed, and played snooker. Mike won every game, but Paul didn't care. He was home by half-past-nine, ready almost to go to bed at once. But he waited for his father.

"How was Aberdeen?" he asked when his father came in.

"Oh, fine, fine." After a moment he added: "I've got to go up again in two to three weeks."

He said nothing more about his trip. Paul, considering it just a work matter, of no concern to himself, soon forgot about it.

On the day school resumed Mike said to him: "Want to come round to my place Saturday afternoon and listen to your team getting beaten?"

Paul started to grin. Celtic were in the Cup Final.

"I wouldn't mind coming round to hear them *win*."

"Some chance of that! Fancy a bet on it?"

"No," Paul said instinctively.

"Christ! What kind of a supporter do you call yourself?"

"A canny one."

"Rubbish! How about five bob on it?"

"Five shillings?" Paul exclaimed. It was half his weekly pocket-money.

"Yes, five bob."

Paul was reluctant, but he couldn't see how he could back out: "OK. Five bob it is."

And, like primary schoolchildren, they licked and intertwined their little fingers to seal the bet.

As he cycled towards Mike's house on the Saturday Paul wasn't hopeful of retaining the two half-crowns in his pocket. Celtic hadn't won a trophy in eight years; just a few months before they had lost the League Cup Final to Rangers. Today's opponents, Dunfermline, had beaten them in the Scottish Cup Final four years earlier. By a strange coincidence the then Dunfermline manager, Jock Stein, had recently taken over at Parkhead, and results had improved; but Paul wasn't entirely surprised when Mike greeted him, gleefully, with the news that the half-time score was Dunfermline 2, Celtic 1.

Only the second half was covered by a radio commentary, on the Scottish Home Service. With Mike's parents they sat down to listen in the living-room. Six minutes after the interval Celtic equalised, and Paul began to feel a great deal more optimistic. Gradually it became clear that Celtic were gaining the upper hand; corner after corner had Paul on the edge of his seat, groaning with frustration as time and again the moves came to nothing. He felt himself beginning to will on the invisible team, playing thirty miles away at Hampden.

And at last, after their umpteenth corner, Celtic scored with a header from Billy McNeill. In his excitement Paul jumped up, cheering; Mike's parents laughed, and Mike said: "Oh God, there goes five shillings."

He was right. The match ended 3-2, and Celtic had their first silverware since 1957. Triumphant and happy, Paul took Mike round the corner to a café and bought them chips and Cokes out of his winnings. He still showed a handsome profit on the afternoon.

Four days later he was buying Mike chips again, but this time from the Tallies' café in Chapelwell. His father was spending another day in Aberdeen, and Paul had invited Mike out for tea. Since his mother's death he had learned the basics of cooking, but he didn't trust himself to be able to prepare something for a guest; and besides, fish suppers were more fun. They ate in the living-room while watching tv, something which Paul wasn't normally permitted.

Since it was a bright, warm evening they went out afterwards and walked round the village, which Mike hardly knew. As they were crossing the football field he laughed when Paul said: "I used to play here myself, once." Then: "What's so funny about that?"

"I can't imagine you as a footballer, that's all."

"Why not?"

"You're so skinny!"

"Oh, thanks, pal! It wasn't very often. Just sometimes, I was a goalie for the school team." He laughed. "When they were desperate!"

"Did you ever save anything?"

Paul tried to think: "I can't remember. I suppose I must have done." Then seeing Mike grinning he exclaimed: "Hey, you're taking the mickey, aren't you?"

"Why did you give it up?"

"Well – I gave it up when I went to the Academy." The Academy didn't play soccer; instead Paul was forced to try to play rugby, a game which he had grown to hate and despise.

"That needn't have stopped you," Mike said. "You could have played for some other team."

"Naw, naw – I never played for serious."

They wandered on, across the grass.

"I can remember my first day at school," Paul remarked.

"Me too."

Paul sighed.

"I had some good times at Chapelwell school, you know. They were good years."

Mike nodded: "Yeah – it was fun at primary school, wasn't it? Nothing to worry about, in those days."

"Nothing at all," Paul agreed. But as he said it he realised this wasn't true. In Primary Seven he'd been troubled for a while by bullying, something which had never happened at the Academy.

They strolled through the village and back to Paul's house, where they listened to one of his tapes and then watched *Z-Cars* till it was time for Mike to go. Paul's father got home about an hour later: "A tiring day," he told Paul. "But I've got a lot of things sorted out."

"Good," Paul said, not paying much attention. His thoughts were still with Mike; he was imagining what they might do in the summer holidays, places they might cycle to, day-long hikes they might make up on to the Fells and across the moors, where he had never been.

Paul's father waited till the Friday night before he told Paul what was happening. They sat in the living-room; Paul was immediately frightened by the seriousness of his father's expression.

"I've been offered a new job," he said. "It's promotion – big promotion, actually."

"Where?" Paul exclaimed. But he already knew the answer.

"In Aberdeen. In our Aberdeen office."

As he said it he didn't look at Paul; he stared at the blank tv screen.

"You mean we're going to leave Eassord?"

At once Paul realised he hadn't kept his dismay out of his voice. His father said quietly: "Yes. But it's for the best, Paul." He cleared his throat. "There's too many memories here, son. Too many memories." He cleared his throat again. "I'm sure it's what your mother would have wished." At last he looked at Paul. He spoke more confidently: "And in fact it would have happened anyway. You can't turn down a chance like this, you know. They don't come along too often. We'll be quite a bit better off."

"But where will we stay?" Again Paul realised he hadn't been able to control his voice.

"Well, to begin with, we'll be in a flat. The firm are going to help with that."

A flat. It sounded totally horrible, too horrible even to be imagined.

"But fairly soon," his father went on, "I think . . . ". He hesitated, and looked away again. "I think we'll be able to buy a little place of our own." He looked down at the floor. "You see, when your mother died . . . There was quite a bit in life insurance, Paul. I put it away, and it hasn't been touched."

Paul felt nothing but confusion and distress: "When are we going to go?" he asked.

His father looked at him again: "Oh, not till the end of term. I've told the firm I don't want to disrupt your schooling. So the plan is – we move at the beginning of July."

Paul tried to count the weeks. He couldn't. He asked: "How long is that?"

"Nine weeks. A long time yet, Paul." He leaned across and briefly patted Paul on the knee: "But you'll like Aberdeen, you'll see. Just think – you'll be able to go down to the beach every day of the summer holidays. Just imagine that! And you'll soon make plenty of new pals."

Paul couldn't speak. He would hate Aberdeen, he knew

he would, he would hate it from day one. He simply nodded, aware that not since the first weeks of his bereavement had he known misery like this.

And that night, in bed, he cried as he hadn't cried since then. As he had done at that time he buried his head under the pillow, under the blankets, to suppress the sounds he was making, to make sure they couldn't be heard through the thin bedroom walls. He had been born in Eassord, he had lived all his live in Chapelwell, and now he was leaving, it was all going to be taken away from him. Every time this thought recurred his tears began again: he had lost so much, he had lost his mother, and now he was going to lose his friends, he was going to lose Mike – but at this thought a terrible, new, dark stab of pain went through him, so hurtful that for a while it startled him into no longer shedding tears. He was going to lose Mike, the best friend he'd ever had, the friend he'd hoped to spend so much time with, together in the summer. Then the tears came again: but now his whole body, his chest and stomach, started to heave with the sobs he was trying to suppress; and if his father hadn't been just feet away he would have abandoned all his inhibitions and howled and howled and howled.

But the next morning, and through all the following days, he made sure that nothing of what he felt showed in his face or in his manner. The ability to do this was something which, the previous year, he had learned to perfection.

He waited a week before he told Mike. Several opportunities presented themselves, when they were chatting, but every time Paul shied away from raising the subject; he felt it was still too painful for him to talk about.

The next Friday, at break, they were standing together on the terrace at the front of the school, eating chocolate biscuits and looking across the playing fields. A group of Fourth Year girls were standing below them, not far away. Neither of them had spoken for some time when Mike leaned towards him, indicated the girls with a quick nod, and said softly: "Christ, just look at the tits on Liz Imrie."

Paul glanced down. Mike was right, Liz Imrie's blouse was well pushed out at the front.

"Yes," he said casually.

"I tell you," Mike said still more softly, "I wouldn't mind getting a feel of her."

Paul was startled. He had never before known Mike to speak so crudely about a particular girl, as opposed to girls in general. He said, a little sharply: "I thought she was going out with Rob Thomson?". Thomson was in Fifth Year.

Mike frowned.

"So what? I still wouldn't mind a feel. And do you see Mary Buchanan?"

Paul looked down again.

"What about her?"

"What do you mean, 'what about her'? Isn't it fucking obvious?"

Paul straightened up.

"Yes, I suppose so." The conversation was beginning to irritate him. After a moment he went on: "Maybe you should try to bribe them. Offer to show them your model aeroplanes, or something."

Mike turned on him: "What's the matter with you? You're in a right miserable mood all of a sudden."

Paul was taken aback: "Well . . . I've got something on my mind."

"What?"

"I'm going away," Paul said flatly. "I'm leaving Eassord."

Just for a second he thought Mike looked dismayed. Then he was at once all curiosity: "You mean, for good? Why? When?"

Paul answered him, as briefly as he could. When he finished Mike said: "Well, I'm sorry to hear that, Paul. I really am."

"Thanks." Paul felt himself blushing, yet again.

"But not till the holidays, you say?"

"That's right."

"Well, we'll have plenty of fun before then. Won't we?"

"I hope so." Paul blushed deeper as he said it.

"Of course we will." He turned back towards the girls: "Meanwhile, I'd still like to think about the fun I could have here."

Paul watched him. His fair hair stirred in the breeze; his blue eyes, which were concentrated on the group below, had a look Paul had never seen in them before.

"Tell me," Mike said, without changing the direction of his gaze, "do you fancy Anne Louden?"

The question took Paul by surprise: "No."

"Christ, you must do. Everyone does. She's the best looker in Third Year."

"Is she?"

Briefly Mike turned back to him: "Come on, Paul, you're not *that* green."

The bell rang on the wall behind them. Without a word Mike moved ahead quickly, so that he was behind the girls when they came up on to the terrace; he followed them till they turned off towards the Girls' Entrance, and then made his way to the Boys' Entrance. He didn't look round to see if Paul was behind him.

Over the weekend Paul felt more depressed than ever about his approaching departure from Eassord. He wished it wasn't going to happen, he wished his father could have got promotion in his present office, he wished his whole life was somehow different; that all the sadnesses he'd had could be got rid of, could be made to go away, so that everything would be different and he could be happy again, like he'd been when he was a child. Why did things have to change, why in particular did his own life have to have such terrible changes in it?

He found himself thinking again and again about Mike. Mike was supposed to be his best friend; but at one point he wondered if, really, he liked him all that much. As soon as he was conscious of the question it astonished him. Surely they got on very well together? Yet Mike had called him 'green'. Did Mike really think he was green? Maybe, in the end, they didn't have a great deal in common. Maybe he wouldn't miss Mike as much as he'd thought.

But on Monday morning Mike was friendly, and joking, and suggested he come round again soon to his place for more lessons in snooker; and Paul decided that over the weekend he'd just been daft.

That Friday, in the afternoon, he got home from school tired. It was a hot, sunny day, and he planned to go out again in the evening, but right now he simply wanted to relax.

When he had changed out of his uniform he came back downstairs and wondered what music to put on. After a moment's hesitation he went, not to the tape-recorder, but to the record-player, and carefully drew one of his father's records out of its sleeve. Lately he had begun more and more to enjoy listening to the music his father liked, and this recording, of Beethoven's *Pastoral Symphony*, was already one of his favourites. He placed it carefully on the turntable.

As the music began to play he slumped on the settee and picked up his father's paper, from the previous day. This was another new taste he was acquiring, for reading a serious newspaper. But today there seemed little of interest in it, and he turned its pages only glancing over the reports till, on the Parliament page, one word caught his eye.

Suddenly he was reading with no consciousness of the music, no consciousness of the room, no consciousness of anything but the words in front of him. His cheeks and ears burned as he read, and re-read, before he threw the paper on to the floor, crossed to the window, and stood looking out into the sunshine.

Still he had no consciousness of his surroundings. His heart was thumping almost painfully as words, images, ideas, came and went in his mind in chaos, but like a chaos behind which there was an explanation so dark, so horrible, that it could not be thought about.

The paper reported that on Wednesday the House of Lords had debated the possibility of legalising homosexuality. A large number of peers, including the Archbishop of Canterbury, had spoken in favour, and at the end Lord Arran had announced that he would shortly introduce a Bill.

This was not the first time that Paul's mind had moved towards a possibility which now, to his horror, he found himself confronting in clearer terms than it had ever presented itself before. Perhaps, one day, a change in the law would make a difference to *himself*.

"No," he said out loud; and then, in his thoughts, he repeated it: no, no, no. He'd had enough bad things happen to him in his life, there couldn't be this as well. He was a late developer, he was 'green' as Mike said; he wasn't interested in girls yet in the same way Mike was, but one day he would be; it was just a matter of time. He was only fifteen, it might be two or three years before he found himself wanting a girlfriend – once he was at university, it could wait till then.

But other images returned to him. Mike in his underpants; Mike stripped to the waist by the Lake of Menteith; handsome boys in the gym, in the swimming pool, on the cricket pitch; all the times when he had *liked looking at boys*. He turned and went to stand behind the settee. He grasped the back of it; and then, abruptly, started to hit it with clenched fists: *I'm not, I'm not, I'm not, I'm not, I'm not, I'm not, I'm not, I'm not*.

As the end of term approached, on July 2nd, the weather seemed to Paul as if it wanted him to remember Eassord, in these final days, as a place of sunlight and heat-haze. One perfect summer's day succeeded another, and as he cycled and walked around the landscape he had known all his life he saw it transformed into an insubstantial world of endlessly changing colours, in which the town lay quietly below its Castle. He could not believe that Aberdeen, or anywhere else,would ever seem as beautiful to him as this space between the steep slopes of the Fetternmores and the more gentle slopes of the Fells, between the eastwards industrial plain with its pit-heads and power stations, and the great western stretch of the Carse, leading out towards the mountains and the beginning of the Highlands.

Time began to pass with unnatural speed. Suddenly it was the last week of term, his last week in Eassord. Paul wandered about Chapelwell whenever he could get a break from helping to fill packing-cases. The dismantling of their home depressed him intensely, and though Tom had come back to help he chose to go off on his own into the long, clear daylight of the Scottish evenings. To his surprise, as he strolled past the places he had known for so many years – the village park, the school, the church, the burn that ran in a hollow of wild flowers, the football field – he felt almost nothing. He had expected to be troubled by painful nostalgia; but he wasn't. He wondered if there was something cold-hearted about him, that he could be so close to leaving Chapelwell and yet hardly be affected by his memories of the place.

The one emotion he did feel, very sharply, also surprised him. For the first time he found himself regretting that his mother had been cremated, instead of buried. He'd always thought he was glad there was no grave, no headstone, no place to visit which could only be a reminder that he would never, ever, see her again. Now, he wished that there was such a place, so that he could have gone to it as if to say cheerio – to have taken, perhaps, some flowers, or a single flower, and left it by her headstone, as a farewell gift.

On the Thursday evening Mike came round for a final tea in Paul's house. His father cooked, and they ate in the kitchen. Paul was ashamed that the living-room was in such a state it was impossible to eat at the dining-table, but Mike didn't seem to mind. To his astonishment, and then rather to his annoyance, Tom was more cheerful and more open with Mike than he ever was with himself; the two were soon joking together as if they were old pals, while Paul and his father ate quietly and listened and laughed.

"Your brother's great," Mike said to him when they went out for a walk.

"Yes" Paul said.

They walked uphill, rather than down into the village, and then along a path which ran beneath the woods to Chapelwell Quarry, quiet now in the evening. The cliffs of excavated rock loomed up in a gigantic semi-circle; oddly, though it dominated the view of Chapelwell from a distance, the quarry was invisible from the village itself, hidden by the nearer trees and the curve of the hill. The path carried on round this hillside, on its way to another quarry on the far side, but Paul and Mike stopped when they came to the base of a slope of rock, perhaps a hundred feet or more high.

"What's up there?" Mike asked.

"Christ knows," Paul said. "I've never been up there."

"Right, let's climb up now."

"I can't!" Paul exclaimed.

"Ballocks! It's dead easy. Come on" – and he was off, already scrambling up the scree at the foot of the cliff.

Paul had no choice but to follow. To his surprise he found that Mike was right. Though it looked daunting from below, the climb wasn't difficult at all. There were plenty of footholds; it was just a question of clambering from one rock to another. Within a few minutes they were at the top, panting and sweating.

"Brilliant!" Mike exclaimed. "Fucking brilliant! Just *look* at this view!"

They were in a clearing of rocks and grass. The trees of the woods above Chapelwell stopped here about twenty feet short of the cliff edge, but on either side curved round to enclose the space. Apart from some wild flowers, none of which Paul could give a name to, the only vegetation other than grass was a clutch of gorse bushes, twisted backwards by the prevailing winds. Below them, beyond the path they had followed, a herd of cattle grazed in a field; a mile or so further on, almost hidden amongst trees, they could see the turrets of Caerlendrick House, the nearest 'big house' to Chapelwell; to their left the bare muirland slopes of the Fells rose above the Caerlendrick estate; beyond the estate they were looking across the whole Carse, to the entire range of the southern

Grampians. The sun was behind a thin covering of high cloud; the diffused light turned the mountains into a pale outline above the greens and browns of the plain.

"Wow!" Mike said softly.

They sat down, side-by-side, on one of the jutting rocks near the cliff edge. Paul felt no need to speak, and was glad that Mike, uncharacteristically, was silent too. After a while he realised that in his head he was hearing the climax of the *Pastoral Symphony*; the great receding chords seemed to be the perfect description of this view in front of him, receding into the distance without a single blemish, a single intrusion to spoil it.

When, after a long time, Mike did speak, he asked quietly: "Are you sad to be leaving, Paul?"

Paul answered just: "Yes."

Mike continued looking straight ahead. He said simply: "I'll miss you."

Paul knew at once that Mike could not have said anything he more wanted to hear. He had no idea how to reply. The sweetness of the words to him almost frightened him, but he didn't want to think about why.

Mike turned to him: "Still – we can always write, can't we?"

The possibility had never entered Paul's head. Immediately he was enthusiastic: "Yes! Of course we can."

"You can tell me all about Aberdeen."

Paul pulled a face. Mike laughed: "Why that?"

"I'd rather hear about Eassord. You can tell me what's going on at the Academy."

"Yes, I will. Of course I will." He paused, and then spoke with a seriousness Paul believed he had never heard from him before: "You'll like Aberdeen, you know."

"What makes you say that?"

"You will." Abruptly he was his usual self, grinning: "Just think of the fun of being by the seaside all the time. Just think of all the birds you'll see on the beach! You can write to me about them."

Paul couldn't not smile: "That's what you want to hear about, is it?"

"Yeah! Christ, I envy you – loads of birds to ogle every day of the summer, all stretched out in their bikinis. Brilliant!"

"You think that'll make me like Aberdeen?"

"Too sure!"

He looked away, across the view. Paul didn't speak his answer. 'I hope you're right', was what he was thinking. 'I hope you're right.' Mike was talking again: "Maybe we'll meet up at university. Who knows?"

"God – I hadn't thought of that."

"Could happen."

He fell into another silence. From time to time Paul glanced at him; he seemed absorbed in the panorama below them, frowning slightly as his blue eyes stared out towards the mountains.

Gradually Paul realised he wanted to put his arm round him. It would complete his happiness, to be able to put his arm round Mike – to lightly stroke him where his fair hair, growing longer in the new style, curled slightly at the nape of his neck. Both of them were in tee-shirts. Paul gently eased his arm across the gap between them, as if he were simply adjusting his weight. His bare forearm brushed against Mike's. He waited for Mike to edge away from the touch, almost afraid to breathe in case it drew attention to himself. Mike didn't move.

Oh Christ, was this another sign that he was queer? That he could so much enjoy touching a boy? Did he really, really, feel about Mike *that way*? But it didn't make any sense; all he wanted to do was to stroke him, feel the fine lines of his torso, show him affection; he didn't want, he couldn't imagine wanting, anything else.

He turned to look at the view, growing paler as the sun sank towards the mountains to the north-west. Tonight, so close to the solstice, the skies would never be entirely dark; twilight would merge into dawn. Paul decided he wasn't going to let thoughts about queerness or anything else spoil what, right now, he knew he possessed: moments of perfection, moments he would remember all his life.

Tom went ahead by train, to be ready to help them in Aberdeen. The removal van arrived early on Monday morning, and by ten o'clock was filled and on its way. Half-an-hour later, with the back of the car choked with suitcases and boxes, Paul and his father left Chapelwell. They drove into Eassord, through the streets of shops, across the river, and out into Alnebrig, in theory a separate town but in reality the northernmost, and most prosperous, suburb of Eassord; they crossed the River Alne and the road climbed and twisted through a rise, from which Paul looked back at the Castle Rock, the smoke of Eassord, and beyond it, below the woods, the clustered houses of Chapelwell; then, as the car followed the bend in the road, the view was hidden as if a shutter had been drawn across it.

He turned and looked in front again, to the road north to Aberdeen. He did not imagine, on that July morning he could not possibly have imagined, that it would be twenty-two years before he would set foot in Eassord again.

TWO

THE PATHS OF RETURN

Meaulnes, il est temps que je vous le dise: moi aussi je suis allé où vous avez été . . . Mais je suis comme vous: j'ignore le nom de ce château: je ne saurais pas y retourner; je ne connais pas en entier le chemin qui d'ici vous y conduirait.

Alain-Fournier
Le Grand Meaulnes

Meaulnes, it is time that I told you: I too went there, where you have been . . . But I'm like you: I don't know the name of that château; I wouldn't know how to to return there; I don't completely know the path which would take you there from here.

(Translation Graeme Woolaston)

ONE

Paul was getting impatient; the train seemed to be dawdling these last thirty miles of his journey. He'd spent an uncomfortable night – every time he travelled like this from London to Scotland he wondered if the description 'sleeper' wasn't the worst joke in the language – and had been up and dressed before the attendant brought him his cup of tea and biscuits. Now he was in the corridor, by an open window. The chilly morning air – it was April – freshened him and eased his annoyance, but he was still longing for the train to gather some speed.

He glanced at his watch. Less than twelve hours ago he had been sitting with Sally in the Lord Nelson in Brighton, drinking a farewell pint of Harveys Best.

"It's good of you to run me to the station," he said.

"Oh, nonsense."

"You've been a big help." He had stayed overnight with Sally and her husband, after his flat had been cleared and his furniture taken away to go into storage.

"Not at all," Sally insisted.

At this hour on a Sunday evening, shortly after opening time, the pub was very quiet. When they spoke they did so almost *sotto voce* : "I'll miss you," Sally said. "We all will."

Paul smiled.

"I'll be back sometimes, for goodness sake. 'I'm no awa tae bide awa'."

"You what?"

"It's a song. 'I'll aye come back and see you'. I'll spare you my singing."

Sally laughed.

"Well – at least you're going back where people will understand what you're saying."

They talked about the years they had worked together,

here in Brighton; old jokes, old names that automatically made them laugh – "remember him?" – helped to cover the sadness in their conversation. Neither of them mentioned Steve. Paul assumed that in Sally's case it was out of delicacy, which he appreciated. In his own case it was because tonight no other name was more in his thoughts. Right from the day he'd finalised his arrangements to go back to Scotland he'd been aware of the dark symmetry he was creating in his life: his mother's death eighteen months before he left Eassord, Steve's death fifteen months before he returned.

He drained his pint.

"Time we headed up to the station."

As they left the pub he remarked: "I'll say one thing, I shall certainly miss English beer."

"Is that *all* you're going to miss about England?"

He pretended to be pensive: "Well, I can't think of anything else offhand."

"I hate you," Sally grumbled. "I don't know why I ever talk to you. You're the most horrible person I've ever known."

But once he was installed on the London train, with his suitcases and his portable typewriter, she hugged him tightly: "Now, you take care of yourself, you hear?"

"I intend to," Paul said softly.

She waited on the platform till the train pulled out. As he waved to her Paul suspected, not for the first time, that if he'd been straight he and Sally would have had much more than a friendship.

In London he took a taxi from Victoria to Euston. Crossing the city on the dark April evening he was reminded of his first-ever taxi journey here, on the September evening he arrived sixteen years ago. Out of a conscious surrender to superstition he had chosen the date of his return quite deliberately: he had come to England on Monday 27th, and tomorrow, when he arrived back in Scotland, it would again be Monday 27th. As the taxi struggled through the West End traffic he found it hard to imagine, let alone remember, the excitement and the thrill and the fun that London had once represented to him. For a long time now the city had either irritated or bored him, and he had hardly visited it except to cross it like this, as quickly as possible.

At Euston he stood below the train indicator and read the list of stations for the Inverness sleeper. So many times he'd seen the word 'Eassord' there. Tonight, it was finally his destination. If it was hard to imagine the past, it was impossible to imagine the future. He felt as if he was about to walk through a paper wall, with no idea what was on the other side. When he boarded the sleeper and found his compartment he realised he simply could not believe that when he stepped off the train, he would be back in the town he had never revisited since the July morning when he and his father had driven away.

And now the train was drawing close. Or was it? He leaned out of the window on his elbows. He couldn't tell exactly where they were. All the years he'd lived in England, in London and Brighton, he'd travelled up and down the east coast route to Aberdeen. Before that, he'd made the shorter journey between Aberdeen and Edinburgh, where he had been a student. When he travelled from Edinburgh to Glasgow his route had taken him to the south of where he was now; though from one stretch of the line, on clear days, he could see Eassord Castle in the distance. But he hadn't re-entered this country which was beginning to surround him: the centre of Scotland, the borderland of Lowlands and Highlands.

He stood upright again and crossed to the window opposite. And – ah! now he knew where he was; there were the tips of the Fetternmores, seen beyond the fields which rose away from the railway cutting. He began moving from one side of the coach to the other, trying to take in the whole view. And so, gradually, as the train drew on to the plain and at last started to accelerate, he watched the landscape of his childhood re-form around him: the Fetternmores to the north, the Fells to the south, closing towards each other to create the gap dominated by the Castle Rock of Eassord.

He leaned out of the window again, for his first close view of Eassord since he was fifteen. From this angle the Rock seemed symmetrical, a great lava cone covered with buildings, with the modern town spread all around its foot. Behind it, far to the west, the mountains were a hazy two-dimensional outline. But at the sight of the familiar range he felt the first, sharp emotion of his journey. He really was 'coming home'. He twisted his head to try to see Eassord's outlying villages, but the folds and tricks of the land concealed the one he was most wanting to catch a glimpse of.

The train began to brake. Paul went back into his sleeping compartment and hurriedly collected his things. His companion of the night was still asleep in the upper bunk, with only his blond curls visible above the sheets. Paul had been delighted when he discovered that, for the first time ever, he was going to be sharing a sleeper with something young and attractive, who, moreover, once Paul was lying in the lower bunk reading, had stripped to his underpants and carefully washed in the tiny wash-hand basin. And his pants were neat little briefs that showed off his very shapely arse, not the horrible boxer shorts that in Paul's opinion ought to have been banned by law. Trying, not very seriously, to read his book, Paul hoped that the presence of this vision was a good omen for everything he was undertaking with this journey.

By the time he emerged again into the corridor with his suitcases the train was coming to a stop and he had missed the opportunity to discover if the outskirts of Eassord had changed much. The station hadn't: he registered at once its atmosphere, which even as a boy he'd been able to identify, of being more a large country halt than the station of an important town.

But, yes, it *had* changed: there was no ticket-barrier. Paul was briefly disoriented, and then surprised that he could have forgotten that Scottish stations, unlike English ones, were now 'open'. He was crossing the space where there used to be a railing when a voice said: "Hallo, Paul! Are you still asleep?"

He turned: "Anne! I had no idea you were going to be

here!"

"Oh, I couldn't just let you arrive with no-one to greet you. And I thought you might need a hand. I see I was right" – she took his typewriter and a suitcase from him as she spoke.

"I must have got you out of bed horribly early."

"No, no, I'd be up at this time anyway. Some of us have *kids*, you know."

He laughed: "Well, I warned you about that years ago."

They walked out into the station forecourt, and Paul stopped. For a few moments he couldn't speak. For months he had been imagining this moment, the precise moment when he would step back into Eassord; but nothing had prepared him for the intensity of the emotion which now hit him without warning: so many of the buildings in front of him were exactly as he remembered, so many were new; the mixture seemed to him to create a surrealistic townscape: "Christ," he said when he found his voice again. "Christ, Anne, but this is weird. This is weirder than I ever thought."

"I'm afraid," he said once he was seated at Anne's kitchen table, "that for the next few weeks I'm going to be the most colossal bore. All you're going to hear from me is, 'my God, hasn't such-and-such changed?'. Or alternatively, 'my God, do you know such-and-such is exactly the same?'. You'd better be prepared."

Anne, frying him bacon and eggs, laughed.

It was because of Anne that he was in Eassord, because of a single conversation with her the previous autumn. They had met in London, when she was down attending a conference; she was an education adviser with the Regional Council. They had been students together in Edinburgh, but recently, by a chance which both amused Paul and pleased him, Anne and her family had moved to Eassord and become his first link with his native town in almost two decades.

Anne was the wife of a university lecturer, with a teenage son and a younger daughter. Apart from the greying of her hair she hardly seemed any older to him than when they had first met; she preserved an outlook which would have been insufferably optimistic if it hadn't been tempered, always, by practical common sense and the wry sense of humour they shared. As undergraduates they were capable of arguing fiercely – both of them had the weakness of finding it hard to be tolerant of views they disagreed with – but perhaps because of the times they had rowed, rather than despite them, their friendship had endured almost twenty years.

He met her by Leicester Square underground and took her to a nearby wine-bar, self-consciously joking about his 'yuppie' status, though he hated the silly word. He was, in fact, an office administrator in Brighton. Sitting opposite her over their first glasses of white wine he wondered what she made of him physically these days – and more particularly, since this was the first time they had met since Steve's death, if she was detecting any signs in his features of the grief he had been living with, and through, since February. He knew he had lost weight, and since he was still very thin this was something he was going to have to correct. Normally, though, he considered that the skinniness of his youth had developed into an attractive slimness, and since he had aged surprisingly little facially, he had begun, in his thirties, to indulge in a limited vanity about his appearance. His hair was grey at the temples but hadn't thinned at all; in texture it remained what it had always been, uncontrollable and usually untidy.

Anne asked, inevitably, about his writing. He had two books in print, two fantasy novels in which, rather to his own surprise, he had successfully created an alternative world in which he could dramatise themes and preoccupations he couldn't tackle through realistic fiction. In his twenties he had tried writing 'straight' novels, but none of them had satisfied him and none of them had been published. He was now well through the third of his fantasy books, and had already made up his mind what he would do once it was finished.

"Come home?" Anne exclaimed when he told her.

"Yes."

"You want to come back to Scotland?"

Paul laughed; he'd known she would react like this: "Is it really that bad?" he asked, teasingly.

They debated the familiar weaknesses of Scotland for some time, till Anne said: "Well, you know, if you do come back, you can always stay with Hugh and me for a while."

He looked at her in astonishment. "Do you mean that?"

"Of course I mean it. We've a basement flat we sometimes let out, but never for very long. You could easily have it, till you find somewhere of your own."

Paul had to be certain Anne wasn't merely being polite: "Are you sure about that?" he asked.

"Yes. "

He felt as if he had placed the first piece of a jigsaw, but it was a piece with a shape on it he hadn't, till that moment, even imagined. Not only would he be returning to Scotland, he would be returning to Eassord. And suddenly, with blinding clarity, he knew it was what he wanted, he knew it was what would be right for him.

"I may well take you up on that," he said slowly.

"Do!"

They each sipped their wine. When Anne next spoke, her tone was cautious: "This decision to come back – has it to do with . . .?"

Paul understood.

"Yes. Though I first thought about it years ago – before I ever met Steve. And I suppose it's always been at the back of my mind, that one day I'd go home. Lately, I'd been thinking about it again, after we – well, after we sort of half split up."

"Half?" Anne asked quietly.

Paul was aware that there was no exact heterosexual equivalent for the relationship Steve and he had arrived at after seven years: "Well, you know we stopped living together. But we were still more than good friends, but not what you might call 'married', for lack of a better word."

He saw in her eyes that she didn't understand. But they had been friends for so long each of them knew instinctively when not to pry, and that reticence on the part of the other wasn't necessarily meant as a brush-off. Anne nodded, as if to indicate he didn't have to explain further if he didn't want to. He changed the subject slightly: "And Brighton – well, the trouble is, it's really a very small town, and after seven years – there's hardly a square inch of the place that doesn't remind me of Steve one way or another. And honestly, I think we must have drunk in every pub in Sussex in our time!" They both laughed, but Paul was quickly serious again: "You know, for the first time I can understand why my father was so keen to leave Eassord. I'd never really forgiven him for that, till now. But he once said to me, 'there's too many memories here'. And now I know exactly what he meant. Exactly."

Anne nodded again, slowly.

Paul had to wait till he was certain his third book would be published before he could put his plans into action. He had saved his royalties on the first two, and with the advance from the third he had a small, but reasonable, amount of capital at his disposal. By selling his car, by the profit he could make on his flat, by the sums he could occasionally earn from reviewing and features work, and with the added factor of some luck, he believed he ought to be able to survive for about twelve months as a full-time writer. It gave him his opportunity, his 'bridge' back to Scotland. One evening he rang Anne to check if the offer of their basement flat was still open. The following day he handed in his notice at work, and put his flat on the market. Eight weeks later he was in Eassord.

Where his first action, after he had breakfasted, was to lie down on the bed, pull the duvet over himself, and sleep.

The journey out to the house had added to the sense of surrealism which had swept over him when he walked out of Eassord station. Anne and Hugh lived in the northern suburb of Alnebrig; as he sat in the front of the car Paul had followed the exact route he and his father took on the morning they drove away from the town. What made the experience still more disturbing was that once they had crossed the river, and left Eassord proper, nothing seemed to have changed. The road was lined with the same villas, it had the same views to the hills, there seemed to have been no new building whatsoever in twenty years, till, after a couple of miles, they came to the outskirts of Alnebrig and to the university which had opened since Paul's time in the town. Even then the campus was set back from the road, and was only glimpsed behind a screen of trees. Paul felt as if he was in a time-warp, as if he had been carried backwards in a Tardis.

When he woke he lunched on the soup and bread Anne had thoughtfully supplied in 'his' kitchen, and then went out to begin his exploration of this unreal town he had travelled to.

The mundane aspects of everyday life restored his sense of the present, of the reality of 1987. He drew money from a cash-dispenser, he shopped in decimal currency, the televisions in the electricity showrooms were all colour. Yet at every turn he was confronted by the past: not the 1960s, but the decade before, which to him existed as a haze of memories of childhood. Many times in the summers of the late Fifties he had come out here to Alnebrig with his mother and Tom. The outings were special, almost expeditions, involving four bus-rides, and were organised as an unvarying ritual; he would have been confused and disappointed if the pattern hadn't been followed exactly, every time. They took the Alnebrig bus to its terminus, beside the bridge over the Alne which gave the little town its name. There was a waterwheel he had to see, though it never turned and never could turn, since the watercourse which fed the mill had long since been closed off. On the Alne there was a weir he loved to hear the sounds of. They bought ice-creams from a chocolate-coloured café, always the same one, and then walked slowly along the straight, extended main street of Alnebrig, where in those days the tartanry and touristry in the summer shops had been to him amusement and colour, even beauty. Finally there was a park to play in, where Tom could chase him in-and-out among the flower-beds.

It was all still there, every detail of it. As he walked back to the flat Paul realised that if he had come here today with his nephew, Tom's boy, he could have watched *him* delighting in the roaring of the weir, bought *him* an ice-cream, let *him* run loose and wild in the park. The past was not only present, it was reproducible.

After he had unpacked his first groceries in the kitchen he went into the living-room and switched on the portable tv Anne and Hugh were lending him for his stay. The *News* was on; at the sight of the Prime Minister he instantly turned the sound down before her hated voice could offend his ears. He sat watching silent pictures of today, April 27th 1987, but in his thoughts Macmillan was Prime Minister, Kennedy was the controversial, because Catholic, candidate for US President, Sputniks with dogs had been launched and there was talk of a man soon going into orbit, Teddy boys were enraging their elders because they could no longer be called up for National Service and made to get their hair cut – throughout all his teens, he reflected, the cutting of young men's hair had been an obsession bordering on the fetishistic amongst everyone over twenty-five.

Oh God – had he made the most dreadful mistake of his life? All the time he had been preparing for this return he had never doubted, not once, the rightness of the decision he had reached in that single moment in the wine-bar – a moment which he had even begun to think of as 'a flash of inspiration', the recognition of what until then had been unconscious. But now, he doubted. For twenty-two years he had avoided coming back to Eassord, even though during his time in Edinburgh it had been less than an hour away by train. He had sealed off his childhood, locked it into a geographical region which he had treated as almost taboo to enter. Now, he had broken the taboo; he had unlocked and unsealed. Would he have done better not to?

After breakfast next morning he took the bus into the centre of Eassord. At once he was surrounded again by the impression of surrealism which had hit him at the railway station: so much of what he saw was the townscape he knew better than any other, so much was intrusive and disorienting. He began walking around the streets systematically, in widening circles from the town centre. Gradually he brought the sensation of chaos under control: *this* was different because a road had been realigned; *this* was different because a shopping mall had erased a number of small streets; *this* was different because a supermarket had replaced a church; *this* was different because it had been stone-cleaned and extended. Bit by bit he made the town make sense of itself; it was what it was as a result of logical, and deductible, changes. By lunchtime it was no longer irrational to him, no longer so disturbingly unpredictable. When he returned to the shopping-centre which now dominated the heart of the town he realised he was hungry, and ready for a good lunch.

He ate in a quiet pub, following his meal with his first pint of Scottish beer since the Christmas before last. Merely to order it was a pleasure: to ask for a pint of 'eighty', not 'bitter'. And in his change there were not only Scottish notes, but pound notes as well, instead of the horrible little coins the English now used. The beer was dark and good, much heavier than southern beers.

While he was drinking it a group of young workmen came into the pub. Instantly Paul was alert to their presence: one in particular was a real dark-haired beauty, in close-fitting jeans. For several moments Paul admired what was none too subtly suggested, when the boy startled him by speaking to his mates. It was several further moments before Paul could identify what was surprising him. Then he realised that instinctively he had been expecting to hear the accent of the south-east, the flattened vowels which he always found a turn-on in themselves. A Scottish accent! What else would a young man talk with, a hundred miles north of the border? Paul had to control an impulse to giggle. This was going to be a major change in his sex-life, discovering that the talent had a Scottish accent.

He drank some more from his beer. If he had turned as Anglicised as this, maybe it was just as well he had come home before he became totally deracinated. But it was sixteen months since he had last been in Scotland; after Steve's death he had managed to find excuses not to visit either his father and Jean, or Tom and Mary and the kids. Soon, very soon, he would have to make the trip. But that return, unlike yesterday's to Eassord, was one which he knew in advance was going to be painful. He finished his pint, and went out.

He turned into Castlegait and began the long, steady climb of the Rock. The further he walked, the fewer changes he found. The Old Town, below the Castle, had been carefully preserved; it was largely seventeenth-century, resembling, apart from the dramatically different geography, any merchant town of similar date in the Low Countries. Closer to the Castle, as in its famous Palace, the influence changed to Renaissance France. He passed a building which looked like a modest Loire château before emerging on to the Esplanade, where he sat on a low wall looking northwards to the Fetternmores and to Alnebrig. He rested for several minutes, and then crossed to the other side.

Two miles to the south he could just see the red roofs of Chapelwell. Most of the village was hidden by the intervening rise of the Royal Park. But there it was, in his sight again at last. How strange would it be to him when he went there? How 'surrealistic', how much in need of being reduced to order? Or would it, as a village, have remained unaffected by the modernisation which had altered the town? He stood for a long time before turning away to begin descending the Rock. In a day or two he would make his return to where this country of his childhood had its exact focus.

He chose Friday, because it was May Day. Once again he took the bus into Eassord, and then set off walking. He quickly reached the part of town where Mike Elliott had lived; he briefly considered making a detour to see the house again, but decided against it. Nonetheless his mind began to fill with thoughts of Mike, and he walked on in a sentimental, erotic nostalgia. For many years now he had categorised Mike as his 'first love' – his first, so ridiculously virginal, love. What on earth could he be like now, at thirty-seven? *Where* on earth was he? Paul had written to him from Aberdeen, got a reply back quickly, wrote again, and heard nothing more from him. But his image, the image of him at fifteen, remained part of his erotic life whenever he wanted to conjure up semi-memories, semi-fantasies, of his schooldays. He could still get off picturing Mike in the gym or in the showers, or standing in front of the class getting the belt. Three loud cracks, and the handsome blond boy was turning back to his desk, his face as composed as if he had just been stroking a cat rather than taking the sting of leather.

But Paul didn't want, today of all days, to be distracted by thoughts like these, and he deliberately pushed them out of his mind. They could be allowed their return later, in bed. He came to the Royal Park, and went in.

The park had once been a hunting estate for the Kings of Scotland, when they were resident in the Palace in Eassord Castle; now it was open and grassy. Paul started to climb the slope away from the town and within a few minutes had reached the crest where it fell away steeply on the other side. Here he stopped.

In front of him, less than a mile away, was Chapelwell.

And, oh God, it *had* changed. It had changed more, not less, than the town behind him. It was bigger almost beyond recognition, to the extent that it no longer seemed a distinct village, but rather a suburb of Eassord. Where he remembered fields – the fields he'd cycled past to school – he saw an unbroken stretch of houses, at least as many again as there had been in the village when he left. And cutting right through this 'suburb', separating the older part of Chapelwell from the town, was a motorway, the Eassord bypass. Dismayed, Paul followed its line westwards as it curved on to the Carse. He had always thought of himself as having grown up 'in the country', but he could see that if he were a Chapelwell boy today, the countryside would lie beyond the village, not all around it.

Even the setting of the village, below the woods, had changed; the trees were much thinner, and the hillside much more patchy, than he remembered. The harvesters of timber had been busy without, apparently, re-seeding.

It was ugly. The view was ugly, there was no other word to describe it. He moved on quickly, slithering down a muddy path from the ridge and out of the park at the back. He was at a crossroads, where he could choose between the main road into the village, or the low road. He followed the latter, conscious at every step that what used to be a semi-rural backroad was now an urban street.

He stopped again when he came to the motorway. A narrow pedestrian bridge offered him his entrance into Chapelwell. *In Walhall wohne mit mir*. But no rainbow, and 'no gods and precious few heroes'.

Now, at last, the whole village lay in front of him. He could see familiar features: the church, the school, the football field, the council scheme on the hill where he had lived for fifteen years. All he had to do was to walk on, walk another hundred yards, across the bridge, and he would be back.

But he couldn't. He couldn't go on. He stood by a low stone wall, looking, listening to the sounds of the village which reached him over the traffic in front of him – and he couldn't walk on.

What was the matter with him? Here was the centre of his childhood: where he learned to walk, learned to talk, went to school, sledged in winter, played in summer, fought, forgot, got the belt, forgot, played again. And he couldn't go into it.

He began to blush with awareness of his foolishness, as if someone was watching him. He tried to draw on his embarrassment, to turn it into a goad as a substitute for courage. But why did he need courage at all? What was he afraid of? He was worse than a phobic: he couldn't even identify what was frightening him.

But whatever it was, it was blocking the way in front of him as certainly as if it were a physical barrier.

Perhaps he had just come too soon, too quickly after his

return to Eassord. Since Monday his days had been saturated with memories. Perhaps he had gorged himself; it was too much, far too much, to be taken in at once.

Gradually, in his confusion, he resolved on this as the explanation of his fear. He would come back again, after a week or two, once Eassord itself had ceased to be strange and new to him. Then he would be ready to tackle Chapelwell, and face more memories and more adjustments to what two decades had done to the places he had known as a child.

He turned round and began walking back into town. After Chapelwell, there would have to be Aberdeen. Or should he plan the visits the other way round, and leave the village till even later? His father and Tom would both be offended if he didn't soon make the relatively short trip to see them. But then he would have to confront the most painful memories of all: not of his childhood, but of his last visit to Aberdeen two years ago, with Steve. He remembered how Steve had shown him the places of *his* past – his schools, his old home, the cottage where he had first been picked up, at fourteen – and how they had talked about a future trip to Scotland when they would go to Eassord, and Paul would take him to see Chapelwell. Like so much he had hoped for, that would never happen. Yet again renewed grief for his lover filled him as he walked on, past the semi-detacheds and the bungalows.

TWO

Steve, his arms deep in suds at the kitchen sink, was singing:

> "Some day he'll come along,
> The man I love,
> And have a great big dong,
> The man I love . . ."

Paul looked up from the Sunday paper, spread out over the kitchen table:

"It's 'And he'll be big and strong', for goodness sake."

Steve spoke without turning round: "Well, that hardly applies to you, does it?"

Paul went back to the paper, smiling, but stuck for an answer.

"Come to think of it," Steve added, "neither does the other version."

"Shut your trap," Paul retorted.

Steve was fond of singing parodies of songs, having particular fun with one Sixties number:

> "To know, know, know him,
> Is to love, love, love him;
> Just to see his bum
> Makes me want to come . . ."

Or alternatively:

> "Just to feel his dick
> Gives me a hell of a kick . . ."

Or more radically:

> "To know, know, know me,
> Is to love, love, love me;

Just to see me smile
Makes your life worthwhile . . ."

"Can't you *ever* sing that song properly?" Paul complained. But he knew, in those early years of their time together, that this final version was close to being the unqualified truth. Until Steve, the word 'love' had signified to him only pain, humiliation, and loss. At university, in his second year, he had 'fallen in love', helplessly and absurdly, with a heterosexual fellow-student. As a result he suffered what in retrospect he believed was almost a nervous breakdown. At one point it seemed as if he would have to repeat the year, but the mere possibility stimulated him into working again, and he passed his exams.

Out of this experience, however, there was one gain: he finally accepted, at twenty, that he was queer. He did so with no pleasure, but rather with a sense of being resigned to bleakness, of showing the same toughness he had needed at school when he knew he was going to be belted. But this, in due time, yielded to a different evaluation, and at the beginning of his final year – in the Scottish system, his fourth – he decided that after he graduated he would move to London, for the sake of the freer gay life there and because by that time homosexuality had become legal in England but not in Scotland.

London's gay scene gave him sexual release, friends, and fun, but also another self-discovery which dismayed him; one night, with a thin young man in black leather, he learned that he could keenly enjoy sadomasochism. For almost three years the experience remained isolated, its message unwanted and whenever possible denied. Emotionally, there was no happiness for him, merely a series of affairs, if they could even be dignified by that word. Twice again he 'fell in love', only to find that that just compounded the disaster of the inevitable end. After four years, by which time he was growing to hate the city, he moved on, still further south, to Brighton. Here, at last, he found sexual peace. He concentrated purely on physical encounters or relationships, avoiding any kind of emotional commitment beyond cheerful friendship. It worked, for a time.

He had been in Brighton three-and-a-half years when he met Steve. The contact ad in *Gay News* was the first he had replied to for eighteen months. It appeared not long after the New Year when Paul, as always in January, was restless to find some new initiative in his life. On his birthday, in the early evening, he deliberately chose to go carefully through the columns of personal ads. This birthday was more significant to him than most; today he was twenty-nine, he was beginning the last year of his twenties. What was he going to do with it? What could he still make of his life before he was thirty? A sense of disappointment was coming to dominate his whole evaluation of his existence. All his efforts as a writer, for example, had led nowhere, and he had begun to doubt if he had any substantial ability as a novelist; he already intended that his next book, if he could be bothered starting another, would be radically different from the fiction he had written until now.

The two opening words of one particular ad caught his eye:

> Brighton. Scot, 23, student, slim, dark, tired of scene, seeks similar age for companionship and fun. Interested music, walking, politics.

Paul ringed the ad with his pen, and carried on.

Later, sitting at his desk, he composed a brief reply. He gave his age as twenty-five, which he could pass for easily. He assumed that by '23' the advertiser meant he was really twenty-eight or twenty-nine; and besides, the phrase 'tired of scene' suggested someone who was in fact older than his early twenties. It was that phrase which had decided Paul to respond to the ad. 'Tired of scene' was what he himself was becoming, heartily. In his letter he did not say that since his early days in Brighton he had only answered ads which were looking for an SM partner. But his last such relationship had tailed off in mutually accepted boredom, without recrimination, a few months before. It was time to try something different again.

Early one evening, three weeks later, his phone rang.

The date was the one he still considered the most unwelcome in the calendar, which he tried never to use if he could avoid doing so: the anniversary of his mother's death. At the end of the phone was a strange voice, quickly identifying himself as Steve Brodie, the man who had placed the ad. Almost the first thing Paul learned about him was that he was an Aberdonian; the accent was unmistakable: "You're from the north-east, aren't you?" Paul asked after Steve had spoken only a few sentences.

"Aye, just that, I'm a Buchan chiel," Steve answered, making Paul laugh at once, and then hope that Steve was even half as attractive as his voice.

"I'd like to meet you," Steve went on, "when would be convenient for you?"

Bloody hell, Paul thought, this guy doesn't mess about. They discussed various possibilities, finally agreeing on Saturday afternoon; it was three days away.

"Where shall we meet?" Paul asked.

"How about somewhere down the sea-front?"

The suggestion took Paul by surprise. He had been imagining the Rockingham or the Greyhound, the two major gay pubs in the town.

"OK," he said.

"Do you know the Banjo groyne?"

"Yes, it's not far from here."

"Well, let's make it 2.30, at the end of the Banjo." For the first time in the conversation the voice hesitated. "I don't suppose there'll be many other people hanging about at that time."

Paul burst out laughing: "Not in the middle of February, no!"

Paul was there by twenty-five past two, not so much in order to show keenness himself, but because he wanted to see how punctual Steve would be. He was dressed in the style he always selected for these occasions. To appear casually sexy he had chosen jeans which were slightly scruffy but tight. Above the waist he was wearing a floppy pullover – to disguise just how thin he was – and an open-necked shirt, but at present they were hidden by his scarf and his anorak. The day was bright and bitterly cold. An east wind was scything across from the Marina; the groyne, called the Banjo because at the end it opened into a circle, jutted out above choppy waves. Paul leaned against the end wall, arms crossed.

Steve had been right in his assumption that no-one else would be lingering on the Banjo on a day like this; and just before half-past Paul's heart began to beat faster, with nervousness more than excitement, when he saw a tall figure in a long dark coat emerge from behind the locked-up shed of the Volks Railway, turn on to the groyne, and start walking towards him with a rapid, lop-sided gait.

Within seconds, such was his pace, he was in front of Paul, already smiling and holding out his hand: "Paul?"

"Steve?"

The firmness of his hand-clasp confirmed the impression of decisiveness he had given on the phone.

"I hope you haven't been waiting long?"

"No, no, just a couple of minutes."

"Good, I'm glad. It's gey cal to be hanging around here!"

The brief injection of Aberdonian words – 'very cold' – would normally have put Paul at once on his guard. He couldn't stand Scots in England who affected to speak with more dialect than they ever would at home. But as he said them Steve grinned in obvious self-mockery. Paul's instant reaction was that his smile redeemed nearly ugly features. His ears stuck out; his nose was large; his jaw-line angular and crooked. He was tall, at least six inches taller than Paul himself. His dark hair was short – far too short; it added to the impression of a sharp, honed north-easterner, whereas, allowed to grow longer, it could have softened the whole impact of his features.

But his eyes – his eyes were already delighting Paul. They were blue; even in a blond they would have been striking, but combined with such dark hair-colouring they were more than that, they held Paul's attention while he made the usual noises of opening a conversation: "Yes, we could have chosen a warmer place for a rendez-vous!"

"No harm, though?" Steve asked, suddenly no longer smiling.

For the first time Paul did so: "No harm," he confirmed.

Steve turned slightly away: "Where shall we go to get warm?"

"How about walking up town?"

"Fine," Steve said. "Yes, fine."

Steve *was* twenty-three. He was a student at the University of Sussex, in the first of two postgraduate years. After taking a degree in Sociology at Glasgow he had come to Brighton and worked for a year as a hospital porter. Now he was studying for a social work qualification; his intention was to become a Probation Officer. All of this Paul learned over lemon tea and buns in a gay-run teashop in the Lanes. In response he gave Steve a similar resumé of his own life. As a result he found himself faced with an embarrassment he could have done without at a first meeting; but it was of his own creation. He looked down at the table and began re-arranging crumbs from his bun: "I'm actually twenty-nine. I think, in my letter . . ."

Steve, sitting opposite, didn't speak. Paul raised his eyes. Steve started to smile.

"Yes, I was thinking you'd packed rather a lot into a short life." Paul laughed. "But why did you do that?" Steve asked. "I mean, why the white lie?"

Paul looked down again, blushing; the old trouble of his adolescence could still recur at times like this: "Well . . . Force of habit, I suppose." At once he realised this was hardly tactful. "I mean, everyone does, don't they?" Oh God, that was worse. He shut up. But Steve's smile was broader: "Yes, I suppose you're right."

"But you didn't, did you?" Paul said, trying to make quick amends for his blunder. Steve shrugged. Suddenly Paul felt he could risk frankness with this man: "And, be honest . . ." He hesitated. "Would you have rung me up if I'd said I was twenty-nine?"

Steve burst out laughing: "Touché! I don't know, though."

He thought for a moment. "Yes, probably I would. I've had enough of young shits for the time being."

Paul was startled. Steve's blue eyes looked straight across at him, as if inviting him – or even daring him – to ask the reason for the expression of bitterness. He remembered what Steve had put in his ad: 'tired of scene'. An emotional history, so familiar it could be imagined easily, suddenly loomed to give a perspective on the lean features sitting opposite him.

Paul changed the subject: "So – what's it like, this course of yours? Hard work?"

They returned in the direction they had come from, to Paul's flat in a quiet Kemp Town backstreet. When he took Steve's coat from him in the lobby Paul saw for the first time the build of this man he had invited home. He was wearing a dark blue sweater – as if to imitate an Aberdeen fisherman, Paul reflected – and fawn cords. Though he was lean, he was clearly better-shaped and more muscular than Paul himself. Unlike Paul he had chosen loose-fitting trousers for the meeting, so it was impossible to judge how well-hung or otherwise he might be; but as Paul showed him into the lounge he noted with quick pleasure a neat arse. Yet as he invited Steve to take a seat, and asked what he would like to drink, he had no idea whether this afternoon was going to end with a sexual encounter or not, or even if he wanted it to. His first impression of Steve, that facially he was ugly, kept recurring. He was beginning to realise that the attractiveness of Steve's features changed with his mood. In repose they were harsh, off-putting; but the moment he became animated, and more especially when he smiled, a strange kind of distorted handsomeness appeared in them.

Steve asked for tea, and Paul went through into the kitchen to fill the kettle. Coming back to the connecting door he pointed to the rows of cassettes on his shelves: "Put on some music, if you like."

Steve stood up and went to examine the tapes.

"What do you fancy?" he asked.

"Oh, you choose. I like them all." He laughed. "After all, I bought them!"

He turned back into the kitchen, wondering if Steve would understand what he was doing. His tapes covered a wide range of types of music: rock, jazz, folk, classical, romantic. He wanted to see what Steve would prefer, what the word 'music', which he'd put in his ad with no other explanation, meant to him.

He was measuring tea into the pot when the music began: two horns, playing a simple phrase. With immediate delight Paul recognised the opening of Schubert's *Ninth*. It was music he might have chosen himself: melodic, confident, brightening the mood of the afternoon as the daylight faded.

"Is that OK?" Steve asked when Paul came through with the tea-things.

"Fine, fine. What's that you're looking at?"

Steve turned with his extraordinary, transforming smile: "I started nosing in your books. A touch of the homeland here."

He held it up. It was a guide to the castles of the north-east. Paul laughed: "I can see that would appeal to you."

He sat down beside Steve on the sofa.

"I hope you don't indulge in homesickness," Steve said.

"Not specifically for Aberdeen, no."

To Paul's surprise Steve threw back his head with laughter: "I should hope not!"

"Is it really that bad?"

"I thought you knew?"

"Well . . . I only actually lived there – full-time, so to speak for two years."

"There you are, then. I had to put up with it for eighteen. Why did you leave?"

Paul leaned forward to pour the tea:

"To go to university. I didn't so much leave the town, as leave school." He added flatly: "I hated it. I didn't stay into Sixth Year."

"Which one was it?"

Paul named it; in turn Steve told him of his own: "It

wasn't much fun."

"Well, mine was dreadful."

"Rough?"

Paul hesitated. His decision to take advantage of the Scottish education system and go up to university at seventeen had been made on the day when, early in his Fifth Year, he had been given six of the belt. Now, in retrospect, the circumstances seemed ironic, though in his SM experiences he had never once replicated, nor wanted to replicate, the practice of Scottish schools. Even so it had acquired a sexual ambiguity for him which presumably it didn't have for Steve; he confined himself to saying: "The school was pretty rough, yes."

"Mine too."

"But I don't dislike Aberdeen itself," Paul said to change the subject quickly. He handed Steve a cup of tea.

"Well, I do," Steve said.

Paul stopped in mid-movement: "Why?"

Steve shrugged, and smiled slightly.

"Why do you dislike anywhere? Because of bad memories."

Paul leaned forward again and poured his own tea. A huge area of delicacy seemed to have suddenly appeared in front of him. He speculated about an unhappy childhood, a bad family background; when he straightened up he once again changed the subject: "I thought maybe you'd come to Brighton because you liked being by the sea."

Steve raised his eyebrows.

"Well, now. That is *shrewd*. You're quite right. It's the only thing I did miss about Aberdeen."

"What about Scotland generally? Do you ever think about going back?"

"Good God, no. Do you?"

"Yes. Sometimes."

"Why?"

"Well . . ." Paul wished he'd kept his mouth shut. "I haven't always been very happy here."

Steve didn't comment. Paul turned back. Steve was studying him as if half-intrigued, half-amused. Paul felt himself blushing. Nowadays it was rare for this to happen twice in one afternoon, and he was about to try yet another change of subject when Steve said: "I couldn't go back anyway, even if I wanted to."

"Why not?"

"If I become a Probation Officer, I mean. There's no Probation Service in Scotland, not as such. So once I qualify – *if* I qualify," he interrupted himself with a quick laugh, "I'll be committed to staying in England. Forever!" he added, laughing again.

"Does that worry you?"

"Not in the slightest."

God, Paul wanted to say, you really don't suffer from indecisiveness, do you? Instead he said: "Well . . . a career's important, of course."

Christ, he thought, what a wet remark that was. But now Steve was looking round the room; after a moment he asked: "You're not a football supporter, are you?"

It was said with such scepticism that Paul burst out laughing: "Yes! What makes you ask?"

Steve nodded towards the mantelpiece: "The Brighton & Hove Albion fixture list." It was tucked in behind a candlestick. "You're not serious, surely?"

"Serious, surely, I am. What's wrong about it?". Paul had met this reaction so many times before it had begun to become a regular source of amusement in his life.

Steve looked at him and shook his head.

"And there was me thinking, from your books and your tapes, that you were a man of some culture."

"I *am* a man of some culture! And I'm also a football supporter."

Steve smiled: "Nonsense. That's a contradiction in terms." After a moment he added: "Who do you support in Scotland?"

"Well, not Aberdeen, I can tell you."

"You don't have to apologise to *me*."

He looked at Paul again, still smiling. In turn Paul started to laugh: "Celtic."

"Stupid question, really. I should have guessed."

"From my surname, you mean? But I'm not a Catholic, you know." He laughed again. "The number of times I've had to say that over the years . . ."

Steve shrugged: "It wouldn't worry me if you were. I got enough of all that crap when I lived in Glasgow. Four years of it!"

"You should let me take you to see the Albion some day." Immediately he thought: hell, that was presumptuous. But Steve only smiled again, and shook his head: "I don't think so."

Paul, having made the blunder, decided there could be no further harm in carrying on: "You might enjoy it."

"And I might enjoy falling off Beachy Head, but I've no desire to find out."

Paul laughed: "You shouldn't have prejudices, you know."

"Rubbish. Having prejudices is one of life's greatest pleasures."

Paul rocked back on the sofa laughing; when he recovered he saw Steve grinning at him mischievously, mockingly; all his suppressed handsomeness was in his features. At that moment the music reached the climax of the symphony's first movement: the phrase which had opened it, now blazing out from the full orchestra as a proclamation of confidence and joy. Steve's eyes turned towards the speakers. Paul glanced down and for the first time registered that Steve's cords, though not tight, were filled where it mattered. His blue eyes returned to meet Paul's. He was still grinning. Christ, Paul thought, you're sexy. You are *sexy*. I want you, young man.

Two or three months later, lying beside Steve in bed, Paul let his hand slide down over Steve's smooth belly to the crumple of his pubic hair and then to the cock, now soft again, which a few minutes before he had been thrilled to pleasure; it was still moist with Steve's cum and his own saliva. He said: "Your knob is the handle on the door of my happiness."

"Jesus Christ!" Steve exclaimed. "That's the yuckiest thing anyone has ever said to me."

Paul rolled away, grinning up to the ceiling: "Yeah – tacky, innit?"

He rolled back and they kissed, wetly and lingeringly. Paul pushed himself up on one elbow and with his free hand ruffled his lover's short, soft hair: "*You* are the door of my happiness," he said quietly.

After a moment Steve smiled.

"Now you're just being soppy."

Paul's hand ran across Steve's head; his hair was like velvet over the bone.

"So?"

"If you put dialogue like that into your novels, no wonder they don't get published."

Paul punched him in the ribs: "Bastard!"

He was at work, one February morning, when the phone-call came from Steve's boss. Steve had been taken ill, he'd been taken to the County Hospital, could Paul come at once? He knew instantly that Steve was dead. He knew it as clearly as if he had been told – less from the tone of Ken's voice than from his own fear, slicing through him as it had done twenty years before when his father first said to him: "Your Mum's very poorly, Paul, more poorly than we thought."

He drove through the town like an automaton, consciously wondering as he did so that he could obey the compulsion of the car's mechanics, traffic signals, the need for safety, even though his mind was barely in the real world but with the body he knew he would find at his destination.

He was right. Ken broke it to him as gently as anyone could, but Paul wanted to say to him: "I know, just tell me how it happened." Steve had been in the cells below the Magistrates Court, with Probation clients, when he collapsed. A policeman had given him the kiss of life, kept oxygen in his lungs till the ambulance came; the ambulance-men did what they could; but before they reached the hospital, less than a mile up the road, he was dead. All the time Paul had known him, perhaps all his life, he had been harbouring an undiagnosed, unsuspected heart weakness. He could have gone at any time. Their seven years together had depended on the postponement of the failure of a valve.

The funeral, at the Crematorium a week later, meant nothing to him. Even the knowledge that Steve's body was in the coffin was purely cerebral. He hadn't seen Steve dead. He wanted the parting of their ways to be the Sunday evening, three days before Steve died, when he had hugged him as he went out of Steve's flat on the way back to his own.

Besides, at the funeral – conducted by an Anglican priest, though Steve had been brought up as a Presbyterian and become a far more certain atheist than Paul was now – he had no special standing. Steve had never been out to his parents; they had no idea of the place in their son's life of the man who sat, some rows behind them, amongst a group of Steve's friends. They knew him only as someone who had shared a flat with Steve till he bought his own two years ago, and who had come up to Aberdeen on holiday with him the previous summer. They were soft-spoken, gentle Aberdonians. As he talked with them afterwards, trying not to see in their eyes the reflection of his own grief and bewilderment, Paul realised that in a saner world he could have loved them as family of his own.

Diffidently, shyly, they asked Paul if he might be so good, if he wouldn't mind, if he could help clear Steve's flat and arrange its sale . . . It was so difficult for them, living six hundred miles away . . . The very thought of re-entering the flat appalled Paul; but that they should ask, without knowing what they were doing, touched him deeply.

But not so deeply as to cause tears. Not once in the past seven days had Paul cried for Steve. He had begun to wonder if there was something wrong with him, if perhaps he had exhausted his capacity to cry when he was an adolescent.

He was wrong, of course. Four days after the funeral came a date now doubly sad to him: the anniversary of his mother's death, and the anniversary of his first telephone conversation with Steve. And that evening, at last, the tears began, and having begun seemed as if they might never again stop. He wept and wept and wept, but not for Steve, nor for his mother, whose very features he believed he would no longer be able to remember if he didn't have photographs of her. He wept for himself. 'The poor, motherless boy'. 'The man whose boyfriend died.' But now – it was 1986 – he was hardly alone in the second category.

For months afterwards whole tracts of music were closed to him, either because they were unbearably poignant in themselves, or because they reminded him of Steve. But one night, when his grief was physical pain, a crushing tightness round his chest, he put on his stereo the famous Kathleen Ferrier recording:

> What is life to me without thee?
> What is left if thou art dead?
> What is life? Life without thee?
> What is life without my love?

With tears running down his cheeks he went into the bedroom and came back with a small bottle he kept there. It contained tranquillisers which his doctor had prescribed for him. He had used hardly any, finding them to be of no comfort. From the kitchen he brought a glass of water, and then rewound the tape and began listening to the aria again. He tipped the first of the tranquillisers into his hand. All it needed now was two or three gulps, maybe half-a-dozen, and it would be over, the story of Paul O'Neill would be at an end.

He couldn't do it. He longed to, but he couldn't. He saw no virtue in this; he saw it merely as proof that below layers of adult pretence he remained the coward he had been as a boy, always scared to do what anyone with any spunk would do.

At the end of his time in Brighton he performed two rituals, aware that they were quasi-religious, a substitute for the rites of the Church. When he was packing away his things ready to go into storage he deliberately chose the last piece of music he would play in the flat. He turned the stereo's volume up to maximum and let it thunder through the rooms and out of the open windows: the first movement of Schubert's *Ninth*.

And on his final day in the town, after he had lunched with Sally and John, who had put him up the previous night, he excused himself saying he wanted to go for a farewell walk round Brighton. Neither of them, doubtless sensing his wishes, asked to accompany him. He walked down to the Palace Pier and along the Kemp Town seafront, till he came to the Banjo. Since Steve's death, all through the previous summer, he had never once been on it, but now he walked to the end and then turned and leaned against the wall, arms crossed.

He had thought of bringing a flower, a single rose, to drop into the sea in memory of Steve. But to put a rose into the muck and detritus of the English Channel hardly seemed an appropriate tribute to anyone. So he simply stood, watching strollers come and go, and the first Volks trains of the spring rattling along the narrow-gauge electric railway. But in his mind it was a February afternoon eight years before, and he saw a lanky, dark-haired boy appear from behind the shed and walk towards him. At the mental picture he started to smile; Steve had always been ungainly in his gait, and inelegant in most of his movements. Somehow it all fitted with his curiously beautiful ugliness.

To his surprise Paul found that now, when he was less than six hours from catching the London train, there was no sadness in him. He didn't regret that everything he had known here was in the past; rather, he was glad and thankful that it had been, that once in his life he had been loved in return as he loved. He stood for nearly half-an-hour, and then started walking back along the groyne, beginning his return to Eassord.

THREE

"How was Aberdeen?" Anne asked on the morning after he came back from a few days in the city; they had met in the common entrance they shared.

"Not too bad," Paul said. "Dad and Jean, and Tom, don't live anywhere near Steve's old haunts, so I didn't have to pass them, or anything. I went down to the beach once, but that was alright."

Anne nodded. Paul had told her beforehand of his worries about the trip.

"And how were the kids?"

Paul smiled.

"Dreadful, of course. Just as I expected."

Anne laughed: "Of course you did. That's why you took such care about choosing what presents to take up for them."

"That was only to bribe them into being slightly less obnoxious than they might have been otherwise."

Anne laughed again: "I don't believe a word you're saying. Oh, by the way, a parcel arrived for you on Friday." She pointed to it on the hall table.

"Ah!" Paul exclaimed. "Money."

"Money?"

"Books for review. Tedious but timely." He picked up the large, almost cubic package. "This'll be the first money I've made since I came back." He smiled. "You're looking at your rent here."

He went downstairs to the flat he had occupied now for two months. A brand-new word processor rested on a table in the front room; he had sold his old one before he left Brighton, calculating that it would be too difficult to transport safely to Eassord. Another table had papers and notebooks tidily arranged on it. He had begun to plan his next book. It would be set in the same imagined world as his first three, and, like each of them, it would extend the unreal history and culture he had called into being, exploring aspects which had previously been only implied or passed over. He enjoyed this stage in the writing of a book, sketching rather than actually executing.

He opened the package of books for review: three novels and a collection of short stories. He sat down with the first of the novels and read till lunch. By then he knew he would like to review it in the words he often wanted to apply to books which were sent to him, and which he hoped that one day he might find the courage to actually use: 'what idiot put this crap into print?'.

After lunch he went out and took a bus into Eassord. The day was warm and sunny, and he strolled through the town with no particular purpose in mind. Over the past two months it had ceased to be strange to him, 'irrational'; he no longer found the Eassord of the 1980s less real than the Eassord of the 1960s. But today his mind wandered back again to that decade. It was twenty years to the week since he left school. In his wilder moments, especially when drunk, he liked to assert that the summer of 1967 represented the highest peak of human evolution, and that since then the race had been going steadily downhill. In May Celtic won the European Cup, the first British team to do so, beating Inter Milan in a game Paul still considered one of the greatest he had ever seen. In June *Sergeant Pepper* was released, and *A Whiter Shade of Pale* was at No. 1. On his final Sunday as a schoolboy he sat watching the first round-the-world tv link-up by satellite, and heard for the first time – and how odd, now, to think that there *was* such a first time – the Beatles singing *All You Need is Love*. In July Parliament at last completed the legalisation of homosexuality in England, after a three-year struggle. By then Scott Mackenzie was in the charts, singing about San Francisco when it was the city of 'the summer of love', and not of inexplicable plague and death. As if to remind him how remote all this had become, he was confronted everywhere by posters lingering from Margaret Thatcher's third election triumph a fortnight previously.

He had stopped to browse in a bookshop window – with the vanity of any writer, regretting that his name wasn't there – when a voice beside him said: "Hallo, Paul."

Paul turned: saw a short, dark-haired man who was, though he didn't yet know it, four years younger than himself: and at once smiled: "Hallo, Bob. What are you doing out and about at this time of day?"

"On parole from the office – ten minutes allowed for exercise." He laughed. "How are you?"

"Fine." He paused. "Yourself?"

"Fine, too."

Paul glanced away, trying not to smile. Bob was wearing the grey suit appropriate to an accountant; the last time Paul had seen him he had been in black leather. The suit, Paul had already decided, did nothing for him, but then, he couldn't imagine himself *ever* fancying someone in a suit.

"I enjoyed the other week," Bob said.

Paul looked back, wondering if he was blushing.

"Thanks. Yes, I did too." He felt he had better add: "I was planning to ring you again some time."

"Great."

There was a silence. Once again Paul had to fight the impulse to smile. He recognised – God, how he recognised – the awkwardness when two people meet casually after they have played out roles in a sexual scenario.

"Do you fancy coming round to my place again some time?" Bob asked.

Paul nodded.

"Yes, sure."

"Good. Well, how about tonight?"

"Tonight?" Paul exclaimed.

"Why not?"

Paul had never intended to involve himself again so quickly in the type of sex he hadn't practised for nearly eight years. But indeed – why not?

"OK," he said.

"Shall we have the same arrangement as last time? I'm afraid I have to dash. Pick you up at seven?"

"OK," Paul repeated. A moment later Bob was moving off, with a smile. Paul turned back to the bookshop window, bemused. The conversation had lasted barely a minute, but in the course of it he had committed himself to an evening of accepting Bob's orders to strip, change, bend over. Except that they wouldn't be 'orders': they would only have substance insofar as he, Paul, consented to give them such: he would be free to choose at any moment to reduce them to futile words. The ambiguity was the essence of everything that would happen. It was his willingness to submit which would constitute the principal element of Bob's pleasure; and he knew he would submit, he would let Bob do what they had agreed the first time they met was acceptable. The anticipation was already starting to make him hard. He had to wait for the erection to subside before he could walk on, towards the bus-stop.

He had posted off the contact ad during his second week in Eassord. He had always intended to do this once he was in Scotland; it was the obvious way to meet gay contacts when, without transport, he had no easy access to the bars of Edinburgh and Glasgow. It was also the first time since Steve's death that he had made a conscious attempt to find new partners. In his last year in Brighton he had had sex only once, with a man he picked up almost by accident at a party and afterwards 'forgot' to ring again.

He knew before he began to draft the ad that he would orient it towards SM. The inclination had always been part of his sexuality, but not only had he not practised it during his years with Steve, he hadn't even admitted its existence to him. Now, a new inhabitant of his old country, he didn't want any kind of emotionally complicated relationship. Indeed, he didn't want to be 'in love' again ever. Love, he had decided months before, was in his past, with Steve. So, if sex alone was the object, it might as well be gratifyingly sensual sex. He soon found the right, familiar form of words which would signal to those in the know what he meant. He gave his geographical location simply as 'central Scotland', and was therefore delighted to find that by far the most interesting reply was from a man who lived barely ten miles away, in a village to the north of Eassord.

This was where Bob drove him early in the evening. His house was on the edge of the village: modern, detached, with a large, well-kept garden. Paul put down his bag with his gear in the sitting-room and went to the back window. The evening was light and clear; beyond Bob's garden, which was on a descending slope, he could see for twenty miles, to the familiar peaks of the Grampians. From this direction the conical shape of Ben Ledi, almost symmetrical except for what looked like a chunk bitten out of the top of it, dominated the range.

"You have a fantastic view," Paul remarked as Bob came into the room behind him.

"You said that the last time."

Paul turned, smiling.

"God, am I getting boring already?"

Bob laughed.

"No, of course not." He went to a well-stocked drinks cabinet. "What's your anaesthetic?" he asked.

They sat in facing armchairs. Paul's 'anaesthetic' was an Islay malt, diluted slightly with Scottish mineral water. While he and Bob chatted, as yet keeping off the subject which had brought them together, Paul looked round the room. Everything spoke of a prosperity greater than just that of a successful accountant. He knew from their first meeting that Bob had attended a fee-paying school in Glasgow, and he assumed that family money had contributed to the furniture, the decor, the paintings on the walls – mostly bright abstracts, contrasting with the cream and white which dominated the room's colour-scheme.

Bob talked about his work. He was short, lean, and apart from the fact that his hair was starting to thin, which he disguised by keeping it cut short, he looked younger than his years. Paul knew from their first encounter that he had well-shaped muscles, the fruit of a deliberate project of work-outs. As a result he could wear leather well; but at present he was still in the trousers of his working suit, and a collar and tie. The formality didn't surprise Paul. In due course it would fit into the context of what they were going to do, as would his own tee-shirt and jeans.

"And what have you been up to since I saw you last?" Bob asked.

"Not a lot. Working."

"Still planning a new book?"

Paul grinned.

"I'm *always* planning a new book. Yes, I'm deep in plotting, all that sort of thing."

Bob nodded.

"What's it going to be about, this new book?"

Paul disliked talking about his writing, except with close friends.

"Oh – much the same as the ones before it."

Bob nodded again, and shifted in his chair.

"And what have you been up to that needs correction?"

Paul's stomach tensed slightly. So, the business of the evening had begun. He put down his glass.

"Precious little, I'm afraid."

"Well, that's hardly satisfactory, is it?"

They looked at each other. This was the stage in any SM session which Paul found the most difficult to negotiate: the transition from normal conversation into a scenario, into the beginning of role-playing. He felt more acutely self-conscious at this point than at any time later; also, invariably, he had a strong urge to call a halt immediately. Though he knew that throughout all that was going to happen he would be able to stop it if it became too much for him, nonetheless he was beginning to be afraid. But his fear was also the beginning of his pleasure. He needed to be scared, he needed to have the challenge to surmount.

"You're very scruffy," Bob said.

Paul glanced down at himself.

"What do you mean," Bob went on, "by turning up in jeans?"

"They're very smart jeans," Paul countered.

Bob raised his eyebrows.

"That sounded cheeky to me, O'Neill. Definitely cheeky."

Paul said nothing. The switch to the use of his surname indicated that the scene had begun in earnest.

"Stand up, O'Neill," Bob said.

Paul hesitated for a moment, then stood up. This was the most crucial step of all out of normality and into SM. He had surrendered control over his body; it was beginning to do what someone else told it to do.

"I don't think your jeans are so smart," Bob went on "that they wouldn't be improved by a little dusting. I think six of the best is in order, don't you, O'Neill?"

Again Paul hesitated before he said simply: "Yes, sir."

His hesitation hadn't been acted. He genuinely found it extremely difficult, until he became used to it again, to call anyone 'sir'. He could enjoy being addressed by his surname, to place him in a submissive role; it was much harder for him to speak in turn as if acknowledging a superior.

"Good," Bob said. "Go and put one of those dining chairs into the middle of the room there."

As Paul did so Bob stood up. When the chair was in place he said: "Stand behind it."

Paul got into position.

"Now stay there," Bob said, and went out of the room.

He took longer to return than was necessary; he had simply crossed the hall into another room. Paul knew he was being made to wait, he was being given time to get nervous.

When Bob re-entered the room he had a cane in his hands. He drew the curtains over the windows before walking across to stand behind Paul. He said just: "Bend over."

Paul bent, grasping the front legs of the chair for support.

Bob gave him six strokes. They stung, each hurting for a few seconds before the next followed. But they were nothing like 'six of the best', nor were they meant to be; they were intended just to stimulate Paul as the beginning of the session. When he straightened up he smarted to an extent which was only moderately unpleasant.

Bob stood in front of him and looked at him.

"I have a feeling, O'Neill," he said, "that perhaps that caning wasn't very effective?"

Paul understood what he was asking.

"It hurt a bit, sir."

"Only 'a bit', eh? Well, that's hardly satisfactory, is it?". Paul said nothing. "I think we'd better give you another six, without the benefit of your jeans to protect you this time. Eh?"

"Yes, sir, " Paul said quietly.

"Good. Strip to your underpants. "

Paul threw his shirt and jeans over the back of the sofa and turned to face Bob in just his white Y-fronts. At times like these he was grateful that he had aged so little he still had the hairless chest and slim physique of a teenager. Bob flexed his cane between his hands and studied him. With a thrill of satisfaction Paul saw in his eyes his appreciation of the body in front of him.

"Right, O'Neill. Now you're much more appropriately dressed to be taught a lesson. Bend over again. "

When Paul bent he took a firmer hold of the chair's legs than before, bracing himself for the first real pain of the encounter. This time the caning made him wince and gasp, though he knew that Bob was still holding back and not inflicting the hurt he could have done.

Even so, when he stood up his backside stung sharply and at once he wanted to rub it; but Bob said: "Stand to attention, O'Neill. Hands by your side. Straighten your shoulders."

Paul complied. Bob laid his cane on the table, came back, and began slowly to caress Paul's buttocks. At the touch Paul started to harden.

"Yes," Bob said, "your arse is beginning to warm up, O'Neill." He stepped away and gently tugged down Paul's pants at the back – taking care, Paul noticed, not to reveal him at the front; it was too early in the scene for that. "Yes," Bob said again, "your arse is nicely reddened. Smarting, is it, O'Neill?"

"Yes, sir. "

Bob began to caress him again: "But you deserve much more, don't you, O'Neill?"

There was an almost bizarre contrast between the harshness of what Bob was saying and the gentleness with which his hands were moving: his touch was that of an admirer, even a lover, and it was keeping Paul hard.

"Yes, sir."

After a moment Bob softly pulled Paul's pants back up again.

"Very well. For the time being you can stand like this and smart. But keep firmly to attention or you'll find yourself smarting a lot more."

He went over to his chair, sat down, and resumed his unfinished gin-and-tonic, leaving Paul in the middle of the room. Paul didn't object; this was a way of continuing the scene, maintaining his loss of control over his body to Bob, while giving him time to recover from his first canings. The stinging was already fading rapidly.

After a minute Bob stood up, opened a drawer in a bureau in the corner, and pulled out an object which Paul recognised from last time. It was a long, two-tailed strap of the type which until two years previously had been used in Scottish schools; the kind of belt with which Paul himself had been strapped as a schoolboy. Bob came over with it and stood in front of him.

"I remember that the last time you were here you preferred to have your arse tanned with this belt rather than your hands warmed. Isn't that so, O'Neill?"

"Yes, sir."

"Well, I'm going to give you a word of warning. If at any time tonight you present yourself in front of me in the wrong kit I won't give you any choice about holding out your hands. Do you understand?"

Paul understood perfectly.

"Yes, sir."

"Good. Now get all this clutter out of here, go across the hall, and come back in white PE shorts. I think it's time we put you through some exercises. You may relax."

Paul stood easy, and turned. He took his things and

crossed to the room, a small study, where Bob had gone earlier. Being required to change like this out of Bob's sight wasn't, he knew, because of some strange prudery; it was so that when he finally was stripped naked in front of Bob it would be part of the scene.

He took off his underpants and selected from his bag the white cotton PE shorts Bob wanted him to wear. He knew what was going to happen when he went back. Bob's invasion of control over his body would be extended as he ordered him to do press-ups and sit-ups; he would take the role, which to Paul's amusement seemed to come naturally to him, of an impatient and scornful PE master, and then either cane or strap him through his shorts. By now he had fully recovered from his first canings, and could face another.

But as he was about to go out into the hall again he stopped, and thought. He knew exactly why he had declined, last time, to let Bob strap him on the hands. It was one thing to engage in adult play-acting – until his first SM experience in London he had never so much as seen a cane – but it was quite another to choose to re-live his real schoolboy punishments. Bob was the first partner he had had with whom the possibility even arose; the people he knew in England had no interest in what happened in Scottish schools.

Paul went back to his open bag. Bob had skilfully worked into the scene a signal whereby he could shape its progress. He pulled out a pair of red football shorts. If he put them on now, and so appeared in front of Bob in the 'wrong kit', he would be replicating exactly that morning when Maclaren strapped him for not having his swimming-trunks.

Slowly Paul took off his white shorts. Still he hesitated. But why not? After all, he was back in Scotland, where he had taken the belt when he was just a kid. Was he going to be more of a coward now? In an abrupt rush of decision he pulled on the red shorts, turned, and headed back to Bob' s sitting-room.

When everything was over Paul, in his underpants, stood by the window looking across the view to the mountains. It was still broad daylight. Through all his years in England he had never ceased to miss these long, clear evenings of a Scottish June. Now he was home again, to enjoy them. He sipped from a glass of chilled white wine as he listened to Mozart playing quietly on Bob's stereo.

He felt profoundly relaxed. And yet part of his mind contemplated what he had done in the last two hours with astonishment, and intellectual unease. When he arrived he had expected the evening to be similar to the first he had spent with Bob; but it had developed into something much heavier. Not for many years had he explored so far down this by-lane of his psychology, had surrendered so completely to the compulsion to let humiliation and pain lead him to the release of satisfaction, like a sunburst after a storm, at their end.

Bob came over to him. He was in the black leather trousers and white tee-shirt he had worn for their final session. He touched Paul on the shoulder: "Are you alright?"

Paul turned, smiling.

"Yes, fine."

"I didn't go too far at the end, did I?"

Paul shook his head: "No, you didn't, don't worry."

"I was wondering, perhaps . . ."

Paul repeated: "Don't worry! I'd have stopped you if I really wanted to."

"Well, if you're sure . . . Shall we sit down?" Suddenly he grinned. "*Can* you sit down?"

Paul laughed as he crossed the room.

"Of course I can! But do you think I should put on some more clothes?"

"Are you cold?". Paul shook his head. "Then don't, please. You look nice as you are." They sat side-by-side on the sofa. "I can't tell you," Bob went on, "what a pleasant change it is to meet a young man who wears decent underpants, and not those awful boxer shorts."

Paul laughed again, partly at the compliment to his age:

"Thanks."

He put down his glass and looked at his hands.

"It's a long time since I saw *that* on my palms," he remarked. The imprints of Bob's belt were pale blue outlines.

"Honestly," Bob said, "I'm a brute. You shouldn't let me do things like that to you."

"Stop worrying about it!"

They had had two sessions, with a break between them for more drinks and to discuss how the second should proceed. For it Bob changed into his tee-shirt and leather trousers and treated Paul, who was again in shorts, like a trainee on punishment drill. Periods of exercise alternated with times when Paul had to stand strictly to attention. When Bob strapped him in this second session he didn't hold back, as he had done before, on what he was doing; the strokes hurt with all the pain Paul remembered from his schooldays.

As the last part of the scene Bob put a cushion over the back of a chair. When Paul bent over it Bob handcuffed each of his wrists to the chairlegs. Though the position wasn't uncomfortable in itself Paul was genuinely unable to move; but he had agreed beforehand to this.

Bob stood behind him: "Get your legs apart, O'Neill. Wider yet. I want your shorts stretched as tight as a drumskin. Keep going." Paul complied. "OK." He went to an armchair and sat down. "In a few minutes I'm going to teach you one final lesson. While I relax you can think about what your arse has got coming to it." He picked up his drink.

Paul made no effort to break off the scene. There was an element of genuine humiliation in the helplessness with which he was bound, as there had been every time he had bent over or held out his hands or dropped to the floor to do press-ups. But he knew he wanted it, he wanted for a short time in his well-controlled life to be under the control of someone else, however much he retained the final power to halt the arrangement if he had to.

At last Bob stood up.

"OK, O'Neill." He picked up his belt. "It's time to give the seat of your pants a sound dusting." He struck Paul once. "If you've the balls to take it, that is. Well, O'Neill? Are you going to be a man, or do you want me to let you off?"

Paul said quietly: "No, sir."

"Very well, then." He ran his hand over Paul's buttocks: "Not going to be much use to you now, these tight little shorts, are they?"

"No, sir."

The beating was the only one of the session which caused Paul any substantial distress. Bob's belt was heavy, and he laid it on with some force. Gradually Paul came closer and closer to asking him to stop; but as each successive shock of pain faded again his pride intensified that he was keeping silent. By the end he was hard.

Bob stepped back.

"Well, O'Neill. I take it you won't be in a hurry for a repeat of that?"

"No, sir."

Bob tugged down Paul's shorts to mid-thigh. He stroked Paul's buttocks: "A hot little arse." After a moment he added: "You've got a very neat pair of buns, O'Neill."

Slightly startled, Paul said: "Thank you, sir."

"But you took that very bravely."

Paul realised the compliment, strange as it was, was genuine. He repeated: "Thank you, sir."

Abruptly Bob's voice was different.

"Paul, are you OK?"

Paul was taken by surprise by the suddenness with which Bob had ended the scene. He twisted round: "Yes, I'm fine."

"You aren't too sore?"

"No worse than I expected. I'm more numb than sore."

Bob put the belt down.

"Are you comfortable, or could you manage to stay like that for another minute or two?"

"Yes, I could. Why?"

"Because if I don't bring myself off soon, I'm going to

burst my pants."

Paul smiled. Bob lay on the floor behind him and unzipped himself. Paul listened as he began to masturbate: already quickly, and with rapid breaths. He paused once: "Christ, Paul, but you've a lovely arse, you really have."

"Thanks," Paul said, smiling again.

Bob's breathing grew faster and faster till he came with a loud groan, and then lay, his breathing returning to normal, till he said: "Thanks, Paul. Thanks."

He stood up and went to the table, cleaned himself with a tissue, and zipped his trousers. He turned round and ruffled Paul's hair: "You really are brave, you know. I don't think I could have taken that last hiding."

Paul didn't know how to reply. Bob knelt in front of him, unlocking the cuffs. Paul straightened up, his back aching slightly from his having been bent over: "I'm stiff in all the wrong places," he said with a brief grin at the age of the joke as he rid himself of the encumbering shorts.

Bob stood in front of him: "Put your wrists together and let me cuff you again."

Paul was startled.

"Why?"

"Because I'd like to bring you off myself. May I?"

Paul had never been jerked off while his own hands were bound. Immediately the idea excited him: "OK."

Bob handcuffed him and then, standing behind him, took him in his arms and began to finger his cock. Paul hardened: "But I'll come on to your carpet," he said.

"That doesn't matter."

Bob began to masturbate him. Within seconds Paul surrendered to the pleasure of being embraced by this man who had hurt him so much; he felt Bob's torso against his back, the leather rubbing against his thighs and buttocks; "Harder!" he urged, and after a minute, "Quicker!" – then he arched back and cried out as Bob's fingers pumped wave after wave of orgasm down his cock; he cried out again as the sensations faded and he realised that not for a long time had the pleasure gone so deep or suffused so far through his whole body.

Bob held him, kissing his back, till Paul said quietly: "Thanks, Bob."

Bob let him go. He fetched a tissue across: "Let me dry you," he said.

The touch of Bob's hands on his cock and over his belly was as tender as a nurse's. Paul, looking down, smiled.

Bob freed him again from the cuffs: "If you like, you can go upstairs and have a bath. By the time you get back I'll have fixed up some music and drinks for us."

The next morning Bob, dressed again as an accountant, dropped Paul off in Alnebrig on his way to work. As Paul entered the house he met Anne, who started to laugh.

"I see coming back to Scotland hasn't improved your morals!"

Paul was embarrassed.

"We just – we just sat up late talking about books."

"Of course you did. What sort of books?"

Paul grinned.

"Leather-bound ones."

"I see! I'm not sure I want to know any more."

"Don't worry," Paul said as he turned towards the staircase to the flat. He grinned again. "Bob's trying to make a good boy of me."

After breakfast he lay on his bed, stripped from the waist down, and began lazily to masturbate. His thoughts wandered over the previous evening. Though the memories excited him, and he knew they would provide food for his fantasies for several days, the intellectual unease which had troubled him when he stood by Bob's window returned. Could it be right, could it be justifiable, to gratify such a passion for pain? He was ready with a defence: that it was preferable by far to grant such a passion its proper outlet in consensual sex, than to vent it in cruelties in the real world. But the doubts persisted. A dark passion was a dark passion, however much it had to be indulged from time to time to keep it under control. And could he deny that somewhere, in some very important part of his psyche, he was stuck in adolescence? Wasn't he just giving an adult gloss to the schoolboy desire to prove he could 'take it'?

He looked at his hands. The marks of Bob's belt were still clear, if faint. Dear God, to have done that again: to have stood with his hands out for the belt. But it had been necessary. It had been necessary, now he was back in the town of his childhood, not just to act out a fantasy, but to recreate what had happened in reality. He wanked on. His thoughts began to concentrate, on the moments of the strappings Bob had given him.

Suddenly he jumped up, stripped completely, and went to the bag he had taken to Bob's. He pulled out the red shorts he had worn in order to bring on himself the first belting. Back on the bed he wanked with increased pleasure, enjoying the smoothness of the nylon round his cock and remembering how he had felt when he stood in front of Bob as he had once stood in front of Maclaren, naked except for shorts. The memory of the night before began to fuse with the memory of twenty-two years ago. He wanked more and more quickly, till he shot into the shorts and turned on the bed, gasping and sweating.

He lay and let the semen grow cool and sticky. He liked the feel of it, how his wet shorts clung to his pubic hair. But the nature of the eroticism which had provoked the orgasm intrigued him more even than its intensity. It was a long time since he had got off by thinking about being belted. Only once before in his life had such an interest come to the fore and asserted itself, for a short time, with similar strength. The memory was a disturbing one; it had happened in the worst and saddest days after Steve died.

FOUR

The fantasy, when it appeared about a month after Steve's death – when it first, so he felt, took him over as he approached climax – was simple: Steve, in front of his school class, hands up, getting the belt. The moment the orgasm was over – and his instant guilt caused it to fade into unsatisfaction before he had finished ejaculating – Paul was horrified. What was this, what new horror was this?

But the following night, again as his wank reached its climax, the fantasy reasserted itself, this time with the voice of a teacher superimposed – 'Right, Brodie, up' – and Paul climaxed as the belt struck Steve's palm: and, as the night before, was appalled by what was happening even while the semen shot into his fingers.

And the next night the fantasy possessed him yet again. This time Steve was in a school changing-room, being strapped for horseplay in the showers, still naked as he held out his hands. It was a scene Paul had witnessed once at his Aberdeen school: and the thought of the six strokes, and the memory of the sound in the confined room, gave him the surge of his orgasm.

Afterwards he couldn't sleep. He got up and sat, in his dressing-gown, close to the fire in his lounge. He had never known such self-disgust with a wank fantasy; he felt as if his sadomasochism was beginning to deprave him, as if he had defiled the bed he and Steve had shared.

He knew where the origin of the fantasy lay. Early in their relationship he and Steve had talked about their respective memories of Aberdeen, and Paul explained his decision to leave school early.

"You left because you got six of the belt?"

"Yes."

Steve started to laugh: "What a wimp!"

Paul turned to him – they were sitting side-by-side on a

sofa: "What d'you mean, 'what a wimp'?"

"If I'd left school because I got six of the belt, I'd never have got past the three times table."

Paul drew back slightly.

"You are joking, I hope?"

"Not entirely. Well, a bit." He grinned.

Paul already knew this conversation was becoming dangerous for him. But he couldn't stop himself going on with it: "So you got six yourself?"

Steve laughed again: "Of course I did!"

Paul stared at him. What a social history, he thought, was expressed by that 'of course'. But how could Steve find it funny?

"Often?"

"Sometimes. Only at secondary school."

"God, I should hope so! Christ, no wonder you don't like Aberdeen."

"Ach, that's got nothing to do with it." Still grinning, he spoke in dialect: "We Aiberdeen louns didna mak a fuss aboot gettin oor licks, like you saftie *Southerners*."

"'Southerners' be damned!" Paul exclaimed, punching him on the arm.

That night, in bed, Paul felt both more erotically charged and more deeply tender towards Steve than was normal. He already knew something of Steve's unhappy adolescence, and the thought that in addition this body he was caressing had been beaten at school was intolerable – and intolerably exciting.

After that one night Paul deliberately pushed all thoughts about Steve being punished out of his mind. He knew that Steve had no SM inclinations, and he was determined Steve should never find out about his own; in their affair Paul could see no place for practices which might make sense sexually, but couldn't possibly, in his view, co-exist with love.

But now, seven years later, that conversation about the belt had come back to haunt him.

For several nights afterwards he was free of the unwelcome fantasy. And then, as if it were determined to pursue him, inescapable in its seductiveness, it recurred yet again. And this time it took its worst form ever: for, as Paul climaxed, the man wielding the belt on Steve was *himself*.

He lay afterwards in tears, holding the pillow which had used to be Steve's. What kind of a sicko, what kind of a total pervert, could get off by imagining himself beating his dead boyfriend?

In daylight he was able to try to rationalise what was happening to him. It wasn't, he knew, the pain of the victim of a beating he found erotic, but the boy's courage as he took it: his toughness, his manliness. And it was easy, so temptingly easy, to picture the stoicism Steve would have shown when he had to.

And he could work out a theory as to why, now, he had begun to fantasise about Steve as a schoolboy. He couldn't – not once since Steve's death – be turned on by remembering the real man he had loved. As a result, his erotic attraction seemed to have become displaced, back to an idea of Steve as he must have been in the years before they met.

The theory was neat enough; and whether or not it was true, arriving at it as an explanation 'worked' for Paul. The troubling fantasy faded away, and did not return. But Paul knew that his explanation was maybe too neat, too glib. Perhaps there was some part of him, not very deep in his unconscious, which had wanted, for a while, to punish Steve for dying.

Then the nightmares began. Paul had hardly dreamt about Steve after his death – or at least, he never woke remembering that he had done so. But about a month after he fought off the morbid sexual fantasy he started to have such dreams night after night after night. In them he didn't remember their happiness, or the love they had known. In every one Steve behaved as he had done at the times when Paul found him impossible: irritable, cold, cruel. These moods could come over him without warning, and in every nightmare it was this Steve he had to try to cope with. They were so vivid, with such agonising accuracy of detail – often he dreamt they were arguing in the very flat where he was sleeping – that he woke from them believing they were reality: and then had to endure the double pain of having re-lived their quarrels and of knowing, afresh, that Steve was dead.

He became afraid to go to bed; he began to sit up later and later, drinking whisky into the early hours of the morning. At last he went to his doctor, who prescribed the tranquillisers with which, one night, he contemplated committing suicide.

Something in his own chemistry, rather than the pills, put an end to his ordeal. As mysteriously as the nightmares had suddenly begun, they suddenly stopped, and never recurred.

For the first year he and Steve were together their relationship was shaped by the inescapable possibility that it might only be temporary. Steve was a student; there was no guarantee that at the end of his course he would find work locally, and Paul was uncertain how easy it would be for him to follow Steve if he moved away.

At first, when he fell in love with Steve – and within two months of meeting him Paul knew he was more in love than he had ever been in his life – this distressed him. There were times when, bitter and depressed, he wondered if he was fated to have everything he loved taken away from him, if there was some kind of curse on him which would prevent him ever finding lasting happiness.

But gradually these moods became rarer and rarer, till he realised he had learned something which until now had escaped him: how to live for today and not for tomorrow. Today they were happy; this month, this summer, they were happy; the future would be lived when it came, and not in anticipation.

The day when Steve found his first job was the finest day of a superb year for Paul. The job was with the Sussex Probation Service, in Eastbourne; Steve would easily be able to travel from Brighton, and moreover could look forward to being transferred back there within a couple of years. Suddenly their relationship no longer had the shadow of temporariness hanging over it. Three weeks later Paul received the first indication that his latest book, a fantasy he had written at high speed, might be published. It was a further three months before publication became definite, and he signed his first contract as a writer. By then Steve had moved into his flat.

Paul had never known such happiness and he believed he never would again; he felt that at thirty he had found the Golden Age of his life. That summer, the summer of 1980, was cool and wet, but he didn't care a toss. Often he and Steve would walk along the Kemp Town seafront in the face of a westerly gale that might have been normal in March, looking down over a grey and gurly English Channel. But the warmest, most perfect evening could not have made Paul more content as he listened, laughing, to Steve singing one of his absurd parodies:

Once, on a high and windy hill
In the morning mist
Two lovers got pissed
And then they were ill . . .

In his bathroom – or 'their' bathroom, as he supposed it now was – Steve had stuck up two handwritten posters with verse of his own composition. The first read:

There's no better way
To start the day
Than by crapping all your cares away . . .

While the second said:

Start the day with a shite,
And everything will go all right.
Start the day playing with your dong,
And everything will go all wrong.

"'What if you start the day," Paul asked, "playing with someone *else's* dong?"

Steve was instantly a Presbyterian minister: "Then you'll *burrrn* in everlasting hell." He frowned deeply: "That's what we call *the good news*."

They had not lightly made the decision to live together. The arrangement whereby Steve stayed on in his own student accommodation had worked perfectly; they spent every weekend together, spoke on the phone regularly in between, but kept individual spaces for themselves during the week. It was on those weeknights that Paul had written his fantasy novel, at a speed he had never managed before – engaged, productive, revelling in the freedom of his imagination to range beyond a naturalism which now seemed plodding and confining by comparison. He needed no analyst to tell him what the source of his inspiration was. He imitated Steve's taste for daft rhymes:

There's nothing like a shafting
To get a writer crafting;
There's nothing like a fuck
To make him try his luck;
I owe it to your looks
That I can write my books.

The doggerel wasn't entirely meaningless. In the past Paul had always found anal sex either disappointing or downright unpleasant, and he had consented to it only reluctantly. With Steve, for the first time, he enjoyed it.

They thought carefully before Steve moved into Paul's flat. It had been perfect for one person; but how would it be for two? Economics – neither of them, at that time, was on a good salary – ruled out buying a new place for at least a couple of years. The most obvious practical problem was that Paul now had to write in a flat where someone else was watching television, or playing records, or just being around. It was solved by turning a box-room into a miniature study – this was in the days before word-processors demanded space – and here, below a ceiling which prevented him standing upright, at a rickety card-table for a desk, Paul wrote the second of his two fantasy novels. On completion it, too, was accepted for publication. Steve, meanwhile, had matured from the student Paul had met into a conscientious, sometimes careworn, Probation Officer. But he enjoyed his work; and in this way, for another two years, they remained happy.

Eighteen months later, and for the rest of their time together, they were happy again. But in between they came very close to breaking up. They resolved their problems by half-splitting; Steve moved to a flat of his own, and each of them began to have casual liaisons on the side. They returned to the rhythm of the early days of their relationship, spending their weekends together but separating during the week.

It was a familiar model for a gay relationship, and, in their case, it worked. But Paul knew that the crisis had had its origins in something he didn't understand: the cause of Steve's extreme vulnerability to mood-changes. During 'the bad times', as he later thought of them, he despaired of being able to predict in what humour Steve would come home from work. He could leave tense and irritable, and return smiling; he could leave cheerful and return dark, frowning, brooding.

Nor could he talk about what was troubling him. At times he seemed so much like a stranger Paul felt as if he were sharing his flat with a pick-up from a week before, not a lover of three years standing. More rationally, he knew that Steve possessed in exaggeration some of the worst characteristics of the men of their race. He could behave like a caricature of a north-eastern Scot, unable to articulate, maybe even afraid to *try* to articulate, his most important feelings and experiences. Often Paul thought of Lewis Grassic Gibbon's great epitaph for his people at the end of *Sunset Song*: 'though seldom of that love might they speak, it was not in them to tell in words of the earth that moved and lived and abided, their life and enduring love'. Paul could easily recognise in Steve this characteristic of his ancestors. It was 'not in him to tell in words' of his depression, his tempers, or his love.

Since Steve would never talk about the subject at length, Paul had to piece together a picture of his adolescence from fragments of conversations. Sexually, it could not have been more different from his own. Steve had first been picked up, in a toilet in Aberdeen, at fourteen. He had been wearing his school uniform at the time. He was fifteen when he was first fucked; by sixteen, a regular and proficient cottager. As far as Paul could gather he had stopped cottaging before he left Aberdeen, but he never indicated why, after so much early sexual experience, he changed his habits. What he did admit to Paul was that his first fuck was so painful he didn't try anal sex again till he was twenty; in their own sex life he rarely took the passive role, though when he did, he gave no indication that he didn't enjoy it.

Paul often attributed his own sexual problems to the fact that he had been almost unbelievably naive till he was seventeen or eighteen. It was only in his late twenties, with Steve, that he had at last found full erotic satisfaction, and in this he saw the prolonged after-effect of the ignorance of his teens. But Steve's so contrasting history made him question if he was right. Steve had known everything before he began to be an adult, and sometimes Paul wondered if he had known too much too early. And sometimes he wondered if Steve had ever told him the full truth about his adolescence.

Their relationship, Paul realised, was like a conventional marriage which might be happy and fulfilling despite the fact that each partner has a secret from the other. The husband never admits to the wife that he is bisexual, and sucks off boys in the cottages on his way home from work. The wife has never told the husband that the man she loved more than any other, who she believes she was born to love, left her before they met and emigrated to America. Each of them has a glimmering of the other's secret; but neither wants to know more, and they are content together.

Paul's sex-life with Steve was excellent, and included a variety of shared fetishisms. They would shower together in jeans, going down in turn to suck the other off with the wet denim clinging to thigh and buttock. In bed they would often begin with Paul still in his underpants, so that Steve had to pull them down to fuck him. And Paul loved to have Steve in football shorts; he loved to feel his balls and cock inside the tight nylon; and he would climax by coming against Steve's arse with its curves filling out the irresistible smoothness.

But Steve never knew that he was a sadomasochist. Since Steve was neither naive nor stupid Paul guessed that he had some understanding of the fact, though Paul never practised SM even after Steve moved out of the flat; he was too afraid that being caned would leave marks which would still be visible at the weekend.

And sometimes he suspected that Steve had a parallel secret. Paul had seen photographs of him as a young teenager; he had possessed a raw but unmistakable prepubescent beauty. A darkness could come over Steve when he talked about his teens, before, invariably, he changed the subject. There were times when Paul wondered if when he had been picked up at fourteen it really was the first time he had had sex; or, in fact, the first time he had consented to it.

Yet he never seemed more relaxed or, even, more mellow, than during the only holiday they spent together in Aberdeen, the summer before he died. Because Aberdeen trips were family visits for both of them, and because neither had come out to his parents (though Paul had long ago told Tom), there seemed no point in wasting a joint holiday on Aberdeen; those were spent abroad. But in August 1985 they travelled home together, and introduced each other to their families.

To Paul's amusement Tom seemed discomfited not only by the presence of a 'brother-in-law' in his house, but by the fact that his two-year-old son took to Steve as if he were indeed 'family'. What was more startling to Paul was to see how quickly Steve, in turn, adapted to being an 'uncle'. The lean Aberdonian, so often austere in his appearance, began to play with the little boy, lying on the floor next to his Duplo bricks, helping him build a garage for his many cars – the boy was car-mad – as if he had years of experience of this; though in fact he had no brothers or sisters of his own. Watching the tactful gentleness of his lover, his ability to enter instinctively into the child's imaginary world as they played, Paul wondered if he were seeing for the first time the qualities which made him a successful Probation Officer. Mary, heavily pregnant with her second child, sat as if presiding contentedly over this unexpected family group. She was several years younger than Tom, who ('like me', Paul thought) had been in his thirties before he married.

Steve gave Paul what he called 'the Grand Tour' of his Aberdeen. His memories were, of course, far more extensive than Paul's; but if amongst them there were some which were darker than he had ever admitted to Paul, they seemed to have lost any power to make him unhappy. As the days of their holiday passed he even appeared to grow younger, as the lines in his face – he was nearing thirty, and it was beginning to show – relaxed and faded.

One evening they parked on the Prom and looked down, under grey, dreich skies, at the hardly less dreich prospect of a deserted beach.

"Fan I wis a loun," Steve said – meaning, 'when I was a boy' – "the beach used to be packed in the summer."

"On a night like this?" Paul asked drily. Steve laughed: "Don't be facetious! I meant, in the days before people started going abroad for their holidays – this place was like Glasgow in exile during the Fair."

Paul looked sideways at him and smiled.

"You're becoming a nostalgia queen, do you know that?"

"Sod off! You're only jealous."

"Of?"

Steve grinned.

"There were some good times to be had here during the Glasgow Fair." Paul threw up his hands in mock horror. "In fact, there was a *lot* to be had here during the Fair."

"Come on, let's move," Paul said, "before my goolies freeze off."

"I told you you'd be jealous," Steve said as they started walking. "As I recall, your fellow Celtic supporters were the more adventurous lot. The times I've banged my head on a crucifix as I've stood up. . .". He laughed as Paul repeated his gesture of affected horror. In reality Paul was thinking yet again of the extraordinary difference between his own teens and Steve's: "You're incorrigible, do you know that?" he said.

They walked southwards along the Prom till they came to the fishing hamlet of Footdee, passed through it, and emerged at the mouth of Aberdeen Harbour. A support vessel for the oil-rigs – easily distinguished by its flattened stern – was going out on the high tide. Seagulls lazily circled over it, leaving it alone as they would not have left a trawler alone.

They leaned against the wall of the North breakwater, content to fall into a relaxed silence. The cold wind blew Paul's hair awry but hardly ruffled Steve's much shorter, tighter dark hair. He was turned towards the harbour opening, as if lost in contemplation of the lighthouse and the breakwaters and the open sea. Paul remembered the first impression he had had of him, that day when they met by another stretch of sea six hundred miles away: that he looked like a north-eastern fisherman. The impression returned, stronger now than ever before. He seemed completely at home here: in his natural setting, the setting he had been born to occupy.

A poem of Joyce's came into Paul's mind:

> Wind whines and whines the shingle,
> The crazy pierstakes groan . . .

He could only recall fragments of it:

> I touch his trembling fineboned shoulder . . .

But the last two lines he remembered clearly:

> And in my heart how deep unending
> Ache of love!

After a long time he said quietly: "I love you, Stevie boy."

Steve turned to him in surprise.

"What's brought that on?"

"Nothing. I just felt like saying it."

"Ach, you great gowk." But as he turned away again Paul saw he was touched. "You get dafter with every passing year, O'Neill." His lips began to curve into a smile. "I suppose you expect me to return the compliment?"

"And are you going to?"

Steve's smile became full: "Well, I'll say this for you. You give a decent blow-job."

"My God! Is that going to be my epitaph? Are you going to carve that on my gravestone – 'He gave a decent blow-job'?"

Their laughter disturbed a group of seagulls which had settled near them on the breakwater; they wheeled away, crying, over the choppy grey water.

FIVE

Paul stood at the window of his flat, looking up into the September sunshine.

"They're away, upstairs," he said. "They're off for the weekend."

"Well," Bob said from behind him. "If I'd known that I'd have brought my belt with me." Paul turned quickly. Wearing a leather jacket and denim jeans, Bob was sitting in one of the room's two large armchairs. He grinned. "I could have dealt with you here and now for keeping me waiting. Never mind, they'll sting just as much when we get to my place. "

Paul crossed the room and sat down opposite his guest. He wondered if he should leave it till later to explain how he felt; but decided there was no point in being evasive.

"Bob, I'm sorry, but . . . I don' t want to do anything this afternoon. I'm just not in the mood. I'm sorry."

For a moment Bob' s expression showed his disappointment. Then, almost immediately, he was the polite middle-class Scot: "OK. Of course. If that's what you' d prefer. "

"It is. I'm just – not in the mood," Paul repeated.

Bob's expression changed again: "Paul, are you OK?"

"Yes." He hesitated. "Well – down a bit, maybe. I've been very busy since I saw you last. " It was five weeks since Paul had last had a session with Bob.

"Working? Is that good?"

"Sort of. I've been checking the proofs of my new book – they came through the post last week. It's a pretty tedious job."

"But satisfying, isn't it? I mean, seeing your stuff in print?"

Paul smiled.

"Yes, I suppose so. "

He knew he couldn't explain to Bob why reading the

proofs had saddened him. It was because the job had suddenly made him feel alone; there was no-one specially close to him with whom he would be able to celebrate the book's publication, unlike its two predecessors. The thought reminded him of something else: "And my flat in Brighton has been sold."

"Ah, good. That took a long time, didn't it?"

"Five months. You know what a hassle I had." One previous sale had fallen through at the last minute. "I wish to God the English would reform their bloody conveyancing laws. I don't expect to have half so much trouble when I buy up here. "

"You're going to buy, then?"

"Oh, yes." Paul indicated the room with a wave. "I mean, I'm very comfortable here, but I can't stay on forever. And all my stuff's in store in Brighton – it' s costing me a small fortune."

"But you did well on the sale of the flat, I take it?"

"Oh, yes. The price I got was unbelievable." Paul smiled. "At least I've gained *something* from all those years in the affluent south."

"So where are you going to buy?"

"Here in Eassord. "

"Really? "

"Yes. That way I can commute either to Edinburgh or Glasgow when I get a job – I'm not committing myself to one city or the other."

"You plan to get a job, then?"

"Well, I must." Suddenly Paul laughed. "I may have made a profit on the flat, but hardly enough to retire on!"

"So – in a sense, you're beginning to settle here now?"

Paul nodded. He said simply: "Yes."

Bob was silent for a few moments before he asked, evidently cautiously: "But that's not what's – making you feel down, is it?"

Paul looked at the floor.

"No. It's more the thought . . ." He shook his head. "It's the thought that Brighton is now very definitely in the past. I've burned my boats, crossed my bridges, and all similar clichés. I don't know . . . Suddenly it seems so *final*."

Again Bob hesitated before he put his question: "You're not *regretting* coming back, are you?"

Paul raised his eyes: "Oh, no." But he wasn't certain if this was the truth.

He stood up: "Well, we'd better be going." He checked himself. "At least, I assume . . .?"

Bob also stood up: "Yes, of course. But listen – I've got my camera in the car. I was hoping to take some photos of you."

"Photos?"

"Yes, in some of your gear. If you don't mind."

Paul laughed, to cover his surprise: "Well . . . No, of course not."

"I thought we could go up on to the hills, find a quiet spot, and take some photos there."

"Good God! Is that safe?"

"Nowhere safer! There's no-one else around for miles."

"Well – if you're sure . . ."

"Put some kit on under your clothes, and then all you have to do is strip down when we get there."

Paul laughed again: "OK, I suppose so. Which reminds me, I've got something new, which I think you'll like. Hang on a moment."

He went out of the room and came back holding up for Bob's inspection a green-and-white hooped football jersey – a Celtic jersey. Bob burst out laughing: "I see! Reverting to your tribal loyalties, are you?"

Paul protested good-humouredly: "This is this season's shirt, it's brand-new. See, it's got the date on it." He pointed to the club badge. "This is their centenary season. I predict great things for them this year."

"Well, *I* predict you'll look very good in it. Hurry up and get changed, O'Neill." He burst out laughing again: "Christ, what a Fenian!"

To judge from Bob's reaction the photographic session was a success. Paul posed as a footballer on the grass by a high muirland road, at first with considerable self-consciousness: "I'm too old to be a convincing footballer," he protested.

"Rubbish. Stanley Matthews was still playing in his fifties."

"God, I hope I've got sexier knees at least."

As Bob had predicted, they were completely alone; so Paul let himself be persuaded into changing out of his football kit into just a pair of PE shorts. He did some slow press-ups with Bob crouching down for the shots; then stood on top of a large boulder, one of many by the roadside, while Bob photographed him from behind and in front. Finally, since there was still no-one else in sight, he bent over the boulder with his head down and his legs splayed.

"That's brilliant," Bob said from behind him. "That's great. OK, you can get up now."

"How will you get those processed?" Paul asked as he pulled on his jeans.

"I'll do them myself. You'll have prints within a couple of days. They'll be a sexy little collection, I can tell you."

Paul laughed as he tugged his Celtic shirt over his head: "Get away with you," he said from behind the nylon.

"Not a bit," Bob insisted. "I keep telling you, you really do have the neatest little arse."

Paul tucked his shirt into his waistband and grinned.

"You're bad for me," he said. But he meant the opposite. The session had flattered him out of his low spirits.

They decided to walk on, and enjoy the hills in a more conventional way. They were on a road which crossed a flank of the Fetternmores, to the north of Eassord; the summit of the highest hill in the range rose to their right. Gradually the road levelled out on to a plateau where the sounds of the town and the industrial belt, three hundred metres below, at last faded behind them. Until now they had not quite been out of earshot of the urban world; but here the noise became unable to penetrate the hills' quietness.

They stopped where the road crossed a burn in a hollow and stood by the bridge's parapet, admiring the view westwards to the Grampians. Much of the muirland which sloped away in front of them was boggy, and a dull brown and green, though on higher rises the heather was in flower. But, as ever, it was the mountains which dominated the landscape. Seen from this height they were more awesome even than when seen from the town: they seemed like the rim of the world itself, a great folded-up and carved and rearing finality to the land. In the clarity of the September sunlight they weren't, as so often, apparently two-dimensional: they stood out in their full reality. It was possible to see the changes in vegetation along them, to see clefts and rockfalls and gorges through which burns poured down to feed the Lowland rivers. And it was the intensity of their blueness – the cutting, brilliant blue, along the whole horizon – which created the glory of the view.

After a while Bob asked:

"*Now* are you glad you came back to Scotland?"

Paul simply nodded.

When they were inside Bob's house he said to Paul: "I've got something for you."

He went upstairs and came back with a black leather jacket and a white tee-shirt.

"Change your shirt first," he said. "This is one of mine, but I think it'll fit you."

"What on earth are you up to?" Paul asked.

"Never mind, just do what you're told."

Paul, baffled, changed. Bob handed him the jacket: "Now try this on."

Paul did so. It was the first time he had ever worn a biker's leather jacket; it felt heavy on his shoulders, and stiff at his elbows as he flexed his arms.

"Stand back," Bob ordered. "Yes, I thought so. It fits you perfectly. You can have it – if you want to."

"Have it?" Paul exclaimed. "You mean, to keep?"

"Yes. It was given me by a friend of mine – believe it or not, it was his girlfriend's, but they've split up now and she doesn't want it any more. It's a shade too small for me" – he smiled – "but I thought it would do you. And I was right."

Paul was still amazed: "But – surely a jacket like this is expensive?"

"It would be normally, but I got it for free. So it's yours, if you like it. Go and look at yourself in the mirror."

Paul crossed the room. The image which confronted him startled him: the jacket turned him into someone he hadn't seen before, apparently much better built than he actually was, and, when he frowned to try the effect, rather menacing.

"Good God!" he exclaimed. "I think it suits me."

"Turn round," Bob said. "Yes, it does. It suits you a lot."

Paul flexed his arms again, to try to get used to the stiffness.

"My God, now I'm a leather queen. You're really corrupting me, Bob, do you know that?"

"I'm surprised you haven't had a leather jacket before."

"Well, for one thing I've never been on a motor-bike in my life. And I always thought I was too skinny for leather."

"Well, you're not."

Paul turned to the mirror again. Once more the reflection he saw astonished him. Is this really, he thought, the same Paul O'Neill who was such a sap at school?

"There's still some film left in the camera," Bob said. "Zip up your jacket and I'll finish it off now."

"OK." As he came back across the room Paul wondered if he would believe in this image of himself till he saw it in a photograph.

After a couple of shots Bob put down the camera: "I know what would improve this. Hang on a moment."

He disappeared out of the room and returned with his handcuffs.

"Hold out your wrists," he said.

For a moment Paul hesitated.

"Bob, I'm not sure I want . . ."

"Get on with it, man."

Paul did as he was asked. The cuffs clicked shut on him:

"Too tight?". Paul shook his head.

"Fine." Bob picked up the camera again. "Lower your head. Look down at the floor. That's it, that's great." He took another two exposures and said: "Now put your head back and look right up at the ceiling. Lift your hands, they're blocking the view of your crotch. That's fine, that's brilliant." The camera flashed twice more. "OK, that's the film finished." He crossed the room, put the camera away in his bureau, and sat down.

"Hey," Paul protested, raising his cuffed wrists. "Are you just going to leave me like this?"

Bob looked at him, unsmiling.

"Yes, I think so."

"Bob – I told you back in Alnebrig . . ."

"Very well. I'll release you if you want me to. But do you want me to?"

Paul gazed back at him.

"What happens if I say no?"

"Guess."

Paul realised Bob must have intended this from the start.

"I see."

Bob stood up again and came back to him. His hands went to Paul's crotch; he groped him through his jeans and the PE shorts he was still wearing from the session up on the hill.

"So," he said. "All man in your leather and denim."

His hand moved to Paul's fly. Paul felt the familiar yet always strange sensation of being unzipped by someone else; Bob groped him again, his fingers now able to close round Paul's testicles through the thin cotton.

"When I deal with a young man in leather," he said, "I like to begin by taking him down a peg or two. I wonder if you'll feel so macho when I've got you over my knee spanking your bare arse."

Half-reluctantly Paul acknowledged to himself that Bob was turning him on. He complained: "This isn't fair."

"What isn't, O'Neill?"

"How am I supposed to put up a resistance while you're toying with my knackers?"

Bob burst out laughing and withdrew his hand.

"Honestly, O'Neill, your language can be very vulgar at times. I really think I should put you over my knee right now."

"Put on your leather trousers first."

"Oh! So it's like that, is it?"

Paul nodded. Bob grinned: "Very well then, you little pervert. If that's what you want, that's what you shall have. But stand still."

He undid Paul's jeans and tugged them and the shorts down to his ankles.

"Right," he said as he straightened up. "Now that pretty little arse of yours is bare and ready to be tanned. But I warn you – for putting me to the inconvenience of getting changed, I'm not going to let you up off my knee till your backside's blazing." He grinned again. "I can only hope that the pleasure of my leather trousers will compensate you for the soreness of your bum."

"I'm sure it will, sir," Paul said. Bob laughed as he left the room.

So they were in another session after all; Bob had judged his man right. Perhaps it had been inevitable all along. Already the thought of simultaneously feeling the cuffs round his wrists, the leather beneath his crotch and belly, and the pain of being spanked, was starting to give Paul a hard-on.

It was ten days before he received the photos from Bob: a complete set of prints. He went through them quickly and then put them away, back in their envelope, in a drawer.

When he took them out again in the evening they seemed to him as they had done at first glance: an ineffective attempt at pornography. Deeply embarrassed, he tore most of them into tiny pieces, so small that there would be no possibility of anyone realising their content once they were in his wastepaper basket. He retained only a photograph of himself dressed as a footballer, and the shots of him in his leather jacket before Bob put the cuffs on him. It was an image of himself he was beginning to like; he had already lost his self-consciousness about wearing the jacket around town.

Later still in the evening he took out a photograph album from the drawer where he had put it on the day he unpacked his travelling trunk. All his other albums were in storage in Brighton; this one alone he had judged too precious to leave behind.

Yet he hadn't opened it since he came here. It was the album of the photographs of his childhood. Now he turned the pages quickly till he found the picture he was looking for: a shot of himself as a gawky, skinny footballer, eyes screwed up against the sun, with a crudely-cut fringe of hair falling over his forehead, and wearing a goalkeeper's jersey and a pair of shorts which reached nearly to his knees. He must have been ten or eleven when it was taken, in the football field in Chapelwell.

Beside it he laid the picture Bob had taken of him in his modern shirt and shorts. For a long time he sat comparing the two photographs.

How, he wondered, did *that* boy become *this* man? The gulf between the two seemed unbridgeable: from the naive, inhibited youngster to the man who was happy to dress as a footballer purely to satisfy a sexual fetishism. He studied the features in the photographs. He could barely detect even a facial resemblance between the two Paul O'Neills; if he hadn't known they were the same person, he believed he would not have guessed it.

But he did know it, and the same person was himself. 'Paul O'Neill'. 'Polly', or worse, 'Pretty Polly', he had been taunted with sometimes at Chapelwell School: there had been occasions when he had had to flail out with his fists to try and kill the nickname. Then 'O'Neill' – he remembered the strangeness of being called by his surname when he went up to the Academy, the way it added to the chilling newness of the senior school, and yet how it had also flattered, making him feel older, a proper schoolboy. Now he was 'O'Neill' again in only two contexts: in SM sessions, and as a writer. He had become familiar with the odd sensation that his name had somehow developed a separate existence from himself; he saw it in print, he saw it in bookshops, it went to places he had never been and probably never would go, as if he had sent it out into the world as a child of himself, rather than a reference to himself. 'Paul O'Neill'. It didn't even reflect how he felt about his personal reality, for, though he loved Ireland, he didn't feel in the least Irish; the foreignness of Ireland was part of its very appeal to him.

He turned the pages of the album, seeing this other Paul O'Neill – or perhaps, these others, he changed so much in the years it covered – grow from toddler to schoolboy to early adolescent. The last photograph had been taken in 1963, the summer before his mother died.

In most of them Chapelwell was the background – the village he had been living near for almost five months now, and still hadn't revisited. He remembered that day when he had set out to go there, and turned back when he was within yards of re-entering it.

He had found a stream of excuses to put off the visit. There was plenty of time, he could go any day he wanted, on impulse; Chapelwell might prove deeply disappointing, boring and characterless; it might have changed so much he would find that the village he grew up in didn't exist any more, he would no longer have a home village .

But this was ridiculous. He couldn't go on postponing this confrontation indefinitely. He had to go. He had to be decisive. He closed the album, and downed the last of his whisky. He would go tomorrow. For certain.

He stood westwards of the village, on the road which led out towards Caerlendrick, climbing here as it passed over a final jut of the hill-slopes above the Carse. At the summit there was a fenced-off promontory in the shape of a half-moon, with a long wooden seat from which the landscape could be viewed at leisure. It was known in the village simply as ' the seat', as if there were no other, and Paul had been astonished to find it; it was the same bench which had been here in his childhood, though greatly weather-beaten after a further two decades of exposure to the Scottish climate.

But from this viewpoint, on this bright September day, he saw the Menteith landscape at last arrange itself into the pattern he remembered best – almost, he felt, its proper pattern; the mountains, the Carse, the town, the hills, took their correct places in a huge semi-circle in front of him; now, finally, he had indeed come home. He remembered lines from a poem he had learned at school:

> This is my country,
> The land that begat me ...

But immediately he thought: so what?

He had been in Chapelwell for nearly three hours. Before climbing to the seat he had rested in the village pub, and now he was slightly tipsy from the two pints he had drunk there. But even in the pub the same question had come to him: so what?

At least he believed he had learned why he had turned away from the village five months ago, and why he had delayed so long before coming back. Somehow he must have unconsciously anticipated what he was feeling now – though how to define it, was another matter. Disillusionment? Hardly; he hadn't found the village unpleasant to return to. A sense of loss? That came closer to it, but only to provoke a further question: *what* did he feel was lost?

He had certainly been wrong when he thought the village might have changed out of recognition. The heart of it, the single main street running down from the church and the war memorial, had hardly changed at all: low eighteenth-century cottages and taller Victorian blocks side-by-side and facing each other behind narrow pavements. As he looked along it Paul realised that if he wanted to make a movie about his childhood it could be filmed here without any difficulty. A couple of hours' work disguising the modernised shop-signs, angles chosen to conceal the handful of new houses, and the 1950s could be recreated with total authenticity. But the idea only brought him back to the recurring question: so what? He knew he would never want to do any such thing.

He had sat in the pub with his memories and his new impressions of Chapelwell. One change was that the school had moved, evidently in the late Sixties to judge from the architecture, to a site close to his old home up the hill. He had passed it as the latest generation of Chapelwell kids came out of it, far more brightly and smartly dressed than he and his classmates had ever been in their slipovers and baggy shorts. One or two of them had Walkmans; he remembered his excitement at their age when he first saw and heard a portable radio, when transistors first replaced the valves that used to glow behind the heavy wooden frontages of what until then had always been called wirelesses.

With a shock he realised that these kids could hardly be described as the *next* generation after his own. Even if he had been heterosexual, any children he might have had in his twenties would have left primary school by now. Indeed it was not impossible that some of the younger ones were actually grandchildren of kids who had been at school at the same time as him.

He had looked curiously at anyone he saw in the streets who seemed approximately his own age. It was, of course, virtually certain that neither he nor they would ever recognise each other. 'Paul? It can't be – is it? Paul O'Neill?' No, especially not since he was in leather jacket and jeans. But he couldn't help wishing it would happen; that this village where he had once known everyone at least by sight might, briefly, not be a village of total strangers. In the pub he had wondered if he should talk to the barman: 'I grew up here, you know, I come from Chapelwell'. But no: it would sound like a classic pathetic bar-room gambit, making the barman politely hide the thought, 'not another one'.

The old school still existed, solitary in the middle of its tarmac playgrounds. It wasn't derelict; clearly it had found some new function which Paul could only guess at. It had been built, like so many across Britain, after the introduction of compulsory education in 1870, and was a Victorian horror of huge classrooms with high ceilings, heated by cast-iron ranges fed with coal. On winter mornings the crates of school milk were placed beside them to thaw out – an inefficient process; often lumps of frozen milk were still banging about inside the little bottles when break came. The pupils sat at iron-and-wood forms which were probably part of the school's original fittings, their writing surfaces cut into by the knives of villagers of whom many, no doubt, had been dead even when he was a boy. The seating arrangement was on the system of merit order, from the teacher's right to his left. Halfway through their second-last term the guillotine had fallen which separated those who had passed their eleven-plus and would go up to the Academy from those who – at eleven years old – were told they had failed. Paul could still remember the day it happened, and the headmaster clinically reading out the lists which had arrived from the Education Department. He himself had been close to the top of his class, but never at it, his progress barred by a carrotty-haired boy who managed to combine being top of the class with winning the belting league for getting the most number of strokes in the year.

The same boy, showing a commendable spread of abilities, had also been far more proficient than himself in the very rough form of football which at break-times stormed up and down the boys' playground. The games, Paul realised now, must have been very peculiar, since the playground was on a marked slope. The segregation of boys and girls – strictly enforced – produced some inevitable, and perhaps not wholly undesirable, effects. As he stood opposite the boys' gate he had recognised the corner of the playground in which he had first been educated in 'the facts of life'. It had been done through a smog of dirty-mindedness, but now he wondered if he ought not to be grateful it had been done at all, since in those days no adult ever gave him a hint of a clue about sex.

Other memories of school invaded him. Himself as an infant, joining in 'In and Out the Dusty Bluebells' – though why in the world bluebells should be dusty mystified him now. Learning joined-up writing by using preposterously old-fashioned pens with metal nibs, that had to be dipped into inkwells and then made all the fingers of his right hand blue. The ghastly singing lessons which must have killed music for child after child after child. His utter, almost spectacular, hopelessness at woodwork. Enjoying being class librarian – this was in Primary Five; God, even then, at nine years old, he had loved books. And 'compositions' – essay-writing. All his life figures had been hostile creatures to him, worrying him in Arithmetic as a child and in his office ledgers as an adult. But words – suddenly the memory of those compositions warmed him; here at last he could recognise himself in the boy who had gone to this school; both for young Paul and adult Paul words were fascinating, he loved how he could use them, he loved his own skill in making them express what he wanted to say.

It was almost the only time in the afternoon that he had had that feeling: of re-connection with his own childhood. Perhaps this explained the disappointment he was feeling now, at the end of his visit. He had learned nothing from the afternoon – nothing of importance, at least. When he left the village he would be the same man who had arrived three hours earlier. It was only through the force of his disappointment that he realised he had unconsciously been hoping – for something; in his present confusion of thought he couldn't even define what. Some massive, overwhelming insight into himself, his past, his life?

But he had so many memories of the village they excluded the possibility of 'memory' as a coherent pattern. They were like the secret pictures of James VIII which Jacobites kept in the eighteenth century, which could only be interpreted from one unlikely angle – and in the case of his memories, he was nowhere near working out what that angle might be.

They were a jumble in which infancy and boyhood and adolescence, summer and winter and autumn, were all thrown together. Here was a pavement which had been deep in snow, with one narrow pathway cleared. A boy stood astride it, not letting him pass. They were both four or five. Paul, saying nothing, pushed the other over into the piled snow at the roadside, and he started crying. Was he punished? He could only remember the contempt he felt for the little squawler in the snow.

Here was the burn, in its deeply overgrown hollow. 'The' burn – Paul realised how much the village referred to itself as if it were a complete universe: 'the' burn, 'the' seat, 'the' brae. Did modern kids think of the village in such terms? By the burn was the ancient 'chapel well' which had given the settlement its name. Wild raspberries used to grow among the bushes here. Paul remembered how the little fruits tasted: with a piercing sweetness, far more brilliant than any other raspberries he had ever known.

Here was the field they sledged down in the winter dark. Nothing to see in front but two or three feet of snow, unless there was starlight or moonlight: and the bravado of hurtling down the fifty-yard slide on a steep slope. It would have meant broken bones if they'd veered off and hit a boulder, or overshot into one of the concrete posts at the bottom. They did it over and over again.

Here was a part of 'the woods' – that village 'the' yet again. There was a bare rise, only grassed, not even flowering, about a couple of metres across and half a metre high. When he was very little he'd been told it was a fairy knowe; and now he half-believed that then he'd half-believed it.

Chocolate bars for 6d, bottles of lemonade for 8d, wildly expensive orangeade for 1/ld. Ice-cream cones from the Tallies. Games of cricket against a broken-down wall, dens under thick rhubarb leaves, summer hours of sending twigs floating along the burn. *The Lone Ranger* on tv and in comics. Conkers in the school playground, and dookin for apples at Halloween – did kids still take pleasure in such things? The smell in the air on Bonfire Night: everyone with their own fireworks in their back gardens, and then the baked potatoes extracted from the bonfire ashes. School parties at Christmas, school trips in the summer term, school starting again in August – the rhythm of the year secure and no more questioned than the endless beltings and the shabby, patched-up clothes of so many of the children.

But none of this cohered into anything he could call discovery. What had he been hoping for? If he had come here *à la recherche du temps perdu*, then he had found it. But it had never been lost; he could have recovered any of these memories at any time, anywhere. The problem was, they signified nothing.

And perhaps the explanation was perfectly obvious. Before descending the hill to the pub in the village's main street he had taken the last, and most important, turning of the afternoon, and had stood, very briefly, across the road from his childhood home. It left him entirely unmoved. He saw only what any passer-by would see: a two-storey harled Scottish council house like all the others in Chapelwell, like hundreds of thousands of others across central Scotland. Even he could detect no individuality in it as he looked up at the window of the bedroom where he had slept for so many years, and down again to the living-room window behind a straggle of rose-bushes and a badly maintained privet hedge.

Of all the memories associated with the building only one came to him before he walked on – the memory which had remained utterly clear for him throughout nearly a quarter of a century: of the January morning when he stood beside Tom at that living-room window watching their mother being carried on a stretcher to the waiting ambulance.

Now he stood at the seat, looking out over the one place in the world he could call his own country. And he felt as if he were barred from it forever – barred, at least, from any sense that he was the same Paul O'Neill who had grown up here. The bereavement he had suffered at fourteen cut across his life irrevocably: *nevermore, nevermore*.

Briefly he shook his head, as if the idea could somehow be literally thrown out of his brain. Perhaps it was nothing but self-indulgent romanticism to see an individual fate in his own history; perhaps what he wanted to protest against was simply adulthood itself? Or worse: the reality of life. Why should experience have meaning, why should memories cohere, why think or hope that a pattern, a sustained development, should be apparent in anyone's existence? Life was just a succession of accidents. They happened, and that was that. To believe otherwise, that they were shaped or had a purpose, was to let the idea of God come sneaking back into credibility, trying not to be identified.

Hadn't he learned all this again in Brighton, after Steve died? Did he have to uproot himself from England, come back to Eassord, hesitate for five months before visiting Chapelwell, only to find out this autumn afternoon what he had known all along?

Steve. The thought of Steve always saddened him, but now, in his melancholy, the sadness was sharper than he had felt it in a long time. Whatever shape his life did have seemed to have been given it by death: the two bereavements that marked the end of his childhood, and the end of any sense of being young.

And in the second case, the end – he was certain of this – of love in his life. This was far from being the first time he had had such a thought; but as he turned away from the seat to begin his journey back to Alnebrig it seemed more incontestable than ever. There might still be many pleasures to come, and much to learn, but he would never love again, not as he had done in the days when he and Steve walked together laughing along Brighton seafront.

It would have been difficult for him to have made a prediction which was more spectacularly wrong. A month later, on the evening before Halloween, in a pub in Glasgow, he met Ian.

THREE

PAINTING THE CLOUDS

Fhreagair mi thu: 's e sin an rud
as brìoghmhoire.
                    Tha mi gad fhreagairt
an còmhnaidh . . .

Crìsdean Whyte,
'Uirsgeul'

I answered you: that's the thing
that really matters.
                    Still today
I'm answering you . . .

(Translation Crìsdean Whyte)

ONE

Nearly four years after his return to Scotland Paul still hadn't become re-accustomed to the Scottish winter, and sometimes he wondered if he ever would. It wasn't so much the cold – there had been four mild winters in succession – but the darkness: the oppressively short days around the solstice and the endless greyness of skies affected by west winds off the Atlantic. This impression of enveloping greyness was, he knew, made worse by Glasgow; perhaps if he had stayed in Eassord he might have felt less closed in by the winter, less claustrophobic. But the hassle of daily commuting to work had proved unbearable, and it was two years now since he moved to the city.

He had found this winter, though until February it had been as mild as its predecessors, the more difficult to endure because the previous autumn he had been very close to leaving Scotland. There had been a possibility of a transfer to a post in Amsterdam, a possibility which had come so tantalisingly near to being realised he had begun learning Dutch in anticipation. But it had fallen through; and so on this cold March Monday he was still in the same job, with a publisher who had used to be an independent surviving on a shoestring and was now a branch of a conglomerate surviving by the pleasure of London, or even New York. Nevertheless there were compensations for their change in status: such as outlets in Holland to which transfers might be obtained.

Paul didn't normally drink at lunchtime, but today, as much for warmth as for alcohol, he had come in to the Carnarvon, a pub not far from his office in the West End. He liked it for two reasons: because it was an old-fashioned, unpretentious Glasgow pub, and because it was here that he had met Ian on an October evening three-and-a-half years ago.

He sat with his pint of eighty, doing the *Guardian* crossword. He had changed dramatically in appearance since that evening when, with a similar pint in his hand, he turned to the handsome blond who had joined their group a few minutes before and began single-mindedly chatting him up. As he approached forty his hair had begun to recede rapidly; realising he could no longer go on looking like an overgrown schoolboy he had it cropped into the crew-cut he had worn ever since. Now it was uniformly grey on both temples. Paul didn't mind; he was more appreciative of the fact that his waistline remained unaltered, and that, when he wanted to, he could still get what he wanted.

The crossword today seemed unnecessarily obscure. Bored, Paul raised his eyes from it and looked along the pub. About a dozen men, all obviously working-class, stood round the central bar drinking and talking quietly. Music played loud enough to be cheerful without being intrusive. Paul went back to the crossword, suddenly smiling when he saw the next clue: 'Hunter without deer? (7)'. 'Hunter' was Ian's surname. After all this time Ian remained Paul's single most vivid memory of the Carnarvon, though it was three years almost to the day since he had last seen him before he went off to New York, supposedly for six months. He had written only twice, the second time to announce he had fallen wildly in love, was getting married, and wouldn't be coming back.

For Paul he had become no more than a short-lived part of the past. Yet even now – he raised his eyes from the paper again – he could see Ian standing in front of him here, with his irresistibly sexy grin of a delighted mischievous schoolboy.

He could see Ian standing in front of him, with the grin of a delighted mischievous schoolboy.

The shock of recognition was so great Paul was unable to speak – unable even to exclaim with surprise – unable, for long seconds, to move a muscle: till Ian, laughing, said: "Yes - it's me!"

Paul's speech was released: "What the fuck - ?"

Then his muscles reacted with one simultaneous reflex: he jumped to his feet and with the same reflex was on the point of hugging Ian when he remembered where they were: instead he grasped Ian's shoulders and only then really believed in the solidity of this man who had appeared like a conjuring trick: as if he were afraid Ian might disappear again with equal ease Paul grabbed his hand and felt in response the decisive, warm grip he remembered so well.

"What the fuck are you doing here?" Paul exclaimed. "I mean, how did you know where to find me? I didn't even know you were in Scotland! How long are you over for? How have you been all this time? Are you on holiday?" – he stopped, realising he was sounding exactly like his eight-year-old nephew who tumbled out his sentences like this when he was excited. Ian laughed: "Ah, where shall I start?"

"First let's have a look at you" – Paul stood back and scrutinised the man in front of him. "You haven't changed at all! It's not fair."

"You have, though. I like the haircut."

"Do you?"

"Much better. Makes you look very distinguished."

"Sod looking distinguished. It's meant to make me look sexy."

Ian grinned.

"That as well."

"Flatterer!"

As the first shock of seeing Ian started to pass Paul could notice the differences in him. His face showed the beginning of lines, especially under the eyes; but he still looked far younger than he was – Paul did a quick mental sum; he was thirty-two now. He was wearing a donkey-jacket and jeans; it was clear he had put on a little weight, but not enough to spoil the well-shaped physique Paul remembered vividly. He was slightly shorter than Paul; had hair of tight, profuse blond curls that Paul had both been wildly turned on by and wildly envious of; and grey eyes which, when he was amused as he was now, could shine with almost hypnotic brilliance.

"My God," Paul said. "You're looking well. America's obviously been good to you." Ian simply smiled. "Let me get you a drink, and then you can tell me all about it."

"No – I haven't time."

Paul was instantly dismayed: "No time?"

"I'm actually on my way . . . I called by your office on impulse, I just thought, I wonder if he's still working here – and of course, you are! Your secretary told me you'd gone to the pub for lunch, so I popped my head in the Halt, and you weren't there, and then I thought, I wonder if . . .". His grin became what it had been when Paul looked up to see him in front of him: full of pleasure in his own ruse of appearing out of the blue after three years' absence.

"And you really can't hang on – just for a few minutes? A decent pint again after all these years?"

"No, but there'll be plenty of time, don't worry."

"How long are you over for, then?"

Ian's smile remained at his mouth; but suddenly his eyes were no longer smiling.

"For good," he said.

"For good!" Paul exclaimed. "You mean, you're back to stay?"

Ian's smile disappeared completely. He nodded.

"And what about . . .?" – Paul couldn't remember Ian's wife's name.

"Mary?" Very slightly he shook his head.

"You mean . . .?"

Ian nodded again, looked away, looked back, and half raised his eyebrows.

"Oh, I see," Paul said. "I see." The impact of all this news at once was overwhelming; it was several seconds before he thought to say, "I'm sorry."

Ian shrugged, and was instantly bright again: "I'm actually on my way to look at a flat, that's why I can't hang about."

"You're moving to the West End?"

"Well, I hope so. I'm staying with my parents just now. Can't put up with that for much longer!"

"I'm living in Hill Street these days."

"Hill Street?"

"Yes, I left Eassord ages ago – here, let me give you my phone number." He fumbled in his jacket pocket for his wallet, got out his business card, and wrote his home number on the back. "There you go," he said as he handed it to Ian. "You will ring me, won't you?"

"Yes, I will, don't worry. Give me a few days to settle in."

"Well, even if you don't move straight away – are your parents still in East Kilbride?". Ian nodded. "Well, you could come in from there easy enough some evening, couldn't you?"

Ian laughed.

"I don't see why not."

"For a pint in the Horseshoe," Paul said. "It has to be the Horseshoe!" They laughed together; it had been their favourite pub three years ago.

"Well, I must dash," Ian said, and held out his hand. Paul grasped it for the second time in barely five minutes. "I'll be in touch" – and he turned and was gone.

Paul sat down again. "Well, well, well," he said quietly to himself. He felt as if Ian had passed in and out of the Carnarvon like a whirlwind, leaving behind – what? He picked up his glass, still half full. In the space of a single pint his life in Glasgow seemed to have turned another corner; but towards what, he didn't yet dare to imagine.

"So who is this blond wonder?" Alex asked.

Paul laughed. One of the reasons he enjoyed Alex's friendship was because he was almost the only person he knew who was even more cynical than himself.

"He's a painter. At least, he was when I knew him before. He didn't give me time to ask what he's doing now."

"You mean, an artist painter?"

"Naw, he's an interior decorator. Of course an 'artist painter'!"

Alex poured out two mugs of tea. They were in his large,

light bedsit; Alex, who was in his mid-thirties, was unemployed. It was the Saturday afternoon after Ian's reappearance. Paul had called round in theory on a purely social visit, but in reality to talk over what had happened.

Alex sat down on the bed – Paul was in his one armchair – and handed Paul his tea.

"So how did you meet him, then?"

"It was back when I was living in Eassord. I got a phone-call one evening, would I like to come through to Glasgow and meet up with this group of writers and so on, that coming Friday? They'd got my number through the lit crit network. So of course I thought, why not? And it was very interesting, a lively meeting. Afterwards we went to the pub, when a guy walked in and joined us. And there I was standing next to this absolute Adonis – curls, lovely body, beautiful eyes. It was lust at first sight, believe me."

"And this was Blondie, I take it?"

Paul laughed: "Yes, it was."

"And of course you chatted him up?". Paul merely grinned. Alex went on: "How far did you get?"

"Not very. About two minutes into the conversation he told me about how he'd recently split up with his girlfriend. I thought, *shit*."

"So he's straight?"

"Mostly."

"'Mostly'?"

"At least eighty percent. But twenty percent – not."

"So he's a *bisexual*?"

Paul burst out laughing: "It's amazing how much prejudice you manage to put into the way you say the word 'bisexual'! Yes, he is. I wasn't the first man he'd had, by any means."

Alex put down his tea.

"So you made it with him, after all?"

"Eventually. Not till we'd met several times. Then one evening – it was into the New Year – we went back to his place to share a joint, and maybe that made me bolder than I'd been up till then . . . and maybe it made him easier, too. Either way, we ended up – having fried eggs for breakfast.

I wasn't totally surprised."

"Why?"

"Because it had been obvious to me for a while that he was far too clued up about gayness to be purely straight."

Alex picked up his tea again.

"I see," he said slowly. "So he spent one night with you, and decided to emigrate?"

Paul burst out laughing again: "You cheeky sod! No, I already knew he was going to go to America. He'd got some kind of scholarship or grant or something, for a six-month study visit."

"Doing what?"

"Painting, of course. He had a curious life-history – he's got a first-class degree in Philosophy from Edinburgh. He worked in England for four years, and then he came back to Scotland to study painting at the Glasgow School of Art – apparently it had been his first love all along. When I met him he'd only recently graduated, that summer. And then, as I say, he went off to New York."

"So you only had the one night with him?"

"No, there were more. But not all that many – he left in March. It was just a fling, really. One of those bells that now and then ring."

"And in America he got married?"

"Yes. After he'd been there about four or five months I got a letter from him, saying he'd met this wonderful woman, the love of his life, etc, etc, and he was going to marry her and stay in America. Just like that. And I never heard from him again."

Alex finished his tea and leaned back against the wall behind the bed.

"And now he's back in Glasgow."

"Indeed."

"And naturally you're planning another 'fling'."

"God, no," Paul said at once. "Though I must admit – the thought did cross my mind."

Alex laughed: "Fancy that!"

"For about ten seconds," Paul retorted, grinning. "But no, I would never go back to an affair from the past. That's a certain recipe for disaster, every time."

"Even Blondie?"

"Even 'Blondie'," Paul said, grinning again. "And in fact, for all I know he could already be back with an old *girl*friend."

Alex sat forward: "Was he into SM?"

"Oh heavens, no." Paul laughed. "He's not *that* poly-sexual. No, it was pure vanilla."

"I hope he's careful, though."

"In what way?"

"Well – after being in New York for three years. Of all places."

"Oh, I see." Paul put down his mug and leaned back in his chair. "Christ, I hadn't thought of that. Yes, you're right. You'd practically have to get him to fill in a questionnaire before you could let him into the bedroom."

"So there you are, then," Alex said quietly.

Paul didn't reply. He was considering why it was that such an obvious point had passed him by. Until now he hadn't even tried to imagine Ian's life in New York; his abrupt reappearance in the Carnarvon had created the illusion he was resuming his life in Glasgow exactly where he had left it off. But now that he thought about it, Paul realised for the first time that Ian's voice had had a slight, but inevitable, American tang to it.

Which was much more obvious when Paul heard him on the phone: "What are you doing after work this evening?" he asked, and Paul noticed the drawl of ' wha-at' and ' wo-ork' .

"Nothing much," Paul said. It was three days later, a week and a day after Ian had so disrupted his lunchtime.

"Fancy a quick pint in the Horseshoe? Just a quick pint, though."

Paul laughed: "Why are you in such a hurry?"

"I've got to sort out my move to my new flat."

"Ah, great. Yes, I think I can manage that." He glanced over the paperwork on his desk. "Better make it six o'clock. Does that suit you?"

"Sure does. See you then."

Paul put down the phone, smiling at the 'sure does'.

Yet, when they were sitting face-to-face in the bright, crowded pub, Ian's Americanness vanished again, and he was the Glaswegian Paul remembered so well, down to the pint of eighty he consumed at a speed which suggested he had been parched of Scottish beer during his exile.

"Is that what you meant by 'a quick pint'?" Paul asked wryly. His own glass was still half-full.

Ian grinned.

"My round," he said, standing up.

Their conversation ranged over the three years since they had last met; but soon Paul noticed he was doing most of the talking, as Ian kept bringing the subject back to him: "So, what are you writing these days?"

"Nothing."

"Nothing?"

"If you exempt cash-flow projections and sales analyses. No, I gave all that up as I settled into publishing. Nowadays I don't write, I make money from writing instead."

"Ah, cynic!"

"Well, my last book got turned down – that wasn't long after you left – and by then I had a full-time job, and I was commuting to and from Eassord, and really . . . I just drifted out of it, I guess."

"And of course you'll drift back into it again one day."

"No, I won't. I've got nothing left to write about. And besides, when you spend a fair part of your working life reading other people's manuscripts it tends to put you off the whole idea."

Ian grinned.

"And what about your private life? How's that been, these three years?"

"About as busy as my word-processor."

"Ach, I don't believe that. Do you still . . .?". He met Paul's eyes; suddenly his own grey eyes had a brilliant sheen of mischievous laughter in them, which in turn made Paul burst out laughing: "Yes, when I get the chance.

Which isn't often, these days. My leather's getting so stiff it creaks when I put it on."

"No big romance in your life then, after all this time?"

"No, and no little one either. Except – well, there was one young man who was rather sweet. *Very* sweet, actually. He looked a bit like you, as it happens – blond, grey eyes. But then the fucker pissed off to Greece. Honestly, everyone I get to know in this flaming city seems to leave it. It becomes quite depressing after a while."

"But you're still here."

"Only just."

Ian looked at him in surprise. Paul explained: "Last autumn – that's fall, by the way" – Ian smiled – "there was nearly the possibility of a job in Amsterdam. Yes, you may laugh. That was everyone else's reaction at the time. But it fell through."

"And now?"

Paul shrugged.

"I don' t know. I suppose it's very probable I'll stay here, but . . . ". He looked across the pub to its gleaming Edwardian mirrors, reflecting the lights and shining polished wood of the ornate Victorian interior. "It tends to go in cycles. Every autumn I wish to hell I didn't live in Scotland. Come the spring, I think it's not so bad again."

Suddenly their conversation was turning serious.

"But it isn't just the weather that makes you want to leave, I take it?"

"No . . . The thing is – you must remember, I lived out of Scotland for sixteen years. And it's very difficult . . . In fact, it's impossible. After you've been away that long, you can never quite settle back again. You're never entirely at home."

Ian frowned slightly.

"And how long has it taken you to realise that?"

"Oh, I think I knew within a few months. I went back one day to my home village – the village I grew up in – and . . .". He shrugged again. "I began to suspect it then."

Ian finished the last of his pint.

"All the same – you didn' t leave."

Paul smiled.

"Well, it would have been slightly awkward, wouldn't it? I mean, I could hardly go to and fro the south of England like a ping-pong ball. And it was just after that" – he checked himself; he had been about to say, 'that I met you'. He went on quickly: "It wasn't long afterwards when I got the job. And of course that pretty well decided the issue. So here I still am!"

He sat back.

"But why the hell am I talking about all this to someone who's just *returned* to Scotland, for Heaven's sake? For the second time, moreover! You're beginning to make quite a habit of it, aren't you?"

Ian laughed. Paul pushed back his chair and stood up: "I see you're ready for yet another pint."

"Ah, I might force myself."

Paul picked up his own glass; once again he was half-a-pint behind. He looked at Ian with a mock frown: "Honestly, Ian, you're going to have to *slow down*. You're not in New York now, you know! We take life at a gentler pace over here."

The expression on Ian's face checked him for a moment before he turned and crossed to the bar. As he waited to be served he thought about what he had seen: a smile at Ian's lips, but in his eyes a hurt that had instantly made him regret his crack about New York. Clearly Ian wanted no reminding that he wasn't there.

Yet when he sat down opposite him again Ian was, on the surface, what he had always been to him: blond, handsome, confident. Paul raised his glass as if in a toast: "Here's looking at you, kid," he said.

"'Kid', indeed!"

Paul sipped from his beer.

"You've hardly said a word about yourself, you know. How are you doing?"

Ian looked down at the table. It was some moments before he spoke.

"Well – I'm still a bit mixed up, I suppose."

Paul waited for him to go on. When he didn't he

prompted quietly: "About what, exactly?"

Ian raised his eyes and grinned: "Oh, everything."

Paul played along with the pretence they were joking: "Apart from the meaning of the universe, what else are you mixed up about?"

Ian shrugged.

"Like you said. It's very strange when you come back after being away for a long time."

He didn't continue. Paul commented: "But there's a hell of a difference between sixteen years and three years. And when you came back from England you'd been away for *four* years. And" – but Ian was already shaking his head: "You can't compare coming back from England with coming back from New York City."

"Yes – yes, I see your point. Glasgow must be quite some change after New York."

Abruptly Ian grinned.

"Now, *there's* an understatement."

Paul smiled.

"It must seem very provincial to you now."

"I wouldn't say that, exactly."

"Small? Quiet?". Paul tapped his glass, once again much fuller than Ian's: "Slow?"

Ian laughed; but otherwise didn't indicate his reaction to any of Paul's adjectives. Paul decided he had to take the risk of trying to break down Ian's continuing reluctance to talk about himself: "So why exactly *have* you come home?" he asked.

At once Ian was uneasy; he looked away as if he didn't want to answer. But Paul pressed on: "I mean, I wondered if you had to."

Ian looked back, obviously astonished.

"'Had to'?"

Now it was Paul who was uneasy: "Well, I didn't know if – I mean, after . . . if, perhaps . . .". He was desperate to be tactful: "If perhaps – you no longer had the right of residency in the US."

Ian looked mystified; then he grinned: "I don't see why not. I'm a US citizen, after all."

Paul sat back: "You're an American?" he exclaimed.

"Yes. What's wrong with that?"

Paul sat forward again: "Nothing. It's just" – he hurriedly made a joke of it: "You might have warned me I was drinking with an American, that's all. This could destroy my street cred at a stroke."

Ian smiled more out of politeness, Paul felt, than amusement.

"I had to become an American citizen," he said, "since I was going to live there. They won't let you otherwise."

"I thought . . .". Paul hesitated, and then decided it was absurd for them to go on not mentioning the person who was central to their discussion: "I thought you'd have the right of residency through being married to an American."

To his relief Ian wasn't discomfited that at last they were talking about his wife.

"That's how it was at first. That's why we got married so quickly – I mean, we were already certain we wanted to stay together, we were completely in love. I was crazy about her. I knew that within two weeks of meeting her – two *days* of meeting her, even." Now that the subject had been broached he became fluent on it: "She was just twenty-one then. But fantastically clued up, about everything. She was working in a bookstore – I'm sure you approve of that! But yes, by marrying her I was able to stay on in the US. So we went to a judge, and . . . There we were. Mr and Mrs Hunter. We'd already gotten ourselves an apartment, so everything was looking just fine."

Paul was listening to Ian's voice with astonishment. Now that he was talking about New York his accent was changing dramatically; the American drawl was growing stronger with every sentence.

He shrugged: "But . . . in the end, it didn't work out. Maybe Mary really was too much younger than me, after all. Or maybe, just too different. She's 'a native New Yorker', like the song says. And she certainly knew the score. And I was always – an immigrant." He shook his head. "I loved New York, I still love New York, I'll always love New York, but . . . ". Once again he shook his head. "It's not an easy city to feel at home in. It's brilliant, it's exciting, it's everything you ever heard about it, but . . . ". To Paul's surprise he smiled. "There was always that ' but '."

Paul nodded slowly.

"I see," he said, completely at a loss to know how to respond to this outpouring, so unexpected after Ian's earlier reticence. He was talking again already, standing up as he did so, and grinning: "And like you keep reminding me, we live at a much faster pace over there. Another pint?"

"Just a half this time," Paul said.

He watched Ian standing at the bar. 'We'? Was it a slip of the tongue, or just a joke? But Paul knew why he'd reacted so strongly when Ian said he'd become an American: it abruptly made him seem remote, altered by his years away, no longer the Ian he had known three years ago and drunk with so often in this pub.

Yet, physically, he had hardly changed. Paul leaned back and looked at the setting in front of him: the large, glittering pub – the finest Victorian pub in the city – packed, as it always was, with drinkers lining the long curve of its central bar; and in the middle of them, Ian. And suddenly Paul felt that the Horseshoe had never quite been complete without this short, fair-haired figure in the foreground.

He was as sexy as ever. Until now Paul had been too involved in their conversation to really notice him in that way. But as he stood waiting for their pints Paul admired what Ian's jeans were showing: that he still had the neatest little pair of buns.

When he came back with their drinks Paul asked: "Tell me – are you no longer British, then?"

"No, I've got dual nationality."

"Oh, I see. And are you still a Scottish nationalist?"

Ian grinned and shrugged, clearly meaning: why ask? It was one of the many things they had always had in common. Paul started to smile: "So, you're a British-American Scottish nationalist. No wonder you say you're mixed up."

Ian grinned in a way Paul was beginning to remember

as characteristic of him in the old days: looking down as he did so, almost shyly. He had never been entirely at ease with the kind of banter Paul was used to among gays. Nonetheless an impulse of mischief made Paul carry on: "It's just as well you didn't live in the Deep South then, otherwise you'd have the Confederacy to cope with as well. You wouldn't have a clue what flag to pledge allegiance to."

Ian looked up, grinning more broadly and shaking his head: "You haven't changed, have you?"

"In what way?"

"You're still as bitchy as ever."

Paul leaned back, spreading his hands: "Bitchy? Me? When am I ever bitchy?"

"When are you ever anything else?"

"It strikes me," Paul said, leaning forward again, "that any bitchiness right now is on *your* part."

They started to laugh together. Paul carried on: "Anyway, now that you're back, you Yankee Limey Scot, what are you going to do with yourself? I haven't asked you a thing about your painting."

"Which one?"

"You know what I mean!"

Ian laughed: "I'm taking it up again."

Paul was startled.

"'Taking it up'? Didn't you paint in the States?"

"Sometimes, of course." He shrugged. "It was a bit like you with your writing, I guess. I kind of drifted away from it."

"But you went over for that, didn't you? I mean, specifically to paint?"

Ian smiled quickly: "Yes, there's an irony in that. But you know, other things happened."

Paul suddenly realised there was another question he'd forgotten to put to Ian; without thinking further he blurted it out: "Children?"

Ian shook his head.

"No – not weans, I'm afraid. Just a wife and a job."

Paul was embarrassed by how tactlessly he had asked

the question; he moved on quickly: "Yes, of course, I see. You wouldn't have much time left for painting?"

"No. So when Mary and me – when we separated" – he hesitated again – "I decided the most positive thing I had to do was go back to painting. That's the main reason I've come home. It's much easier to do that over here."

"Over here?" Paul exclaimed. "With our miserable arts funding?"

Ian's grin was suddenly the broadest Paul had seen all evening.

"Do you know anything about arts funding in the *States*?"

Paul nodded, smiling: "Point taken."

"No," Ian went on, "if you're trying to live on a small income, it's much easier to survive over here than in the US."

"With our decadent European social security system, you mean?"

"Something like that! Anyway, I've found myself a flat in Hyndland and a studio in Dennistoun, so now all I need is materials."

"And a bike to get between the two!"

"And as you say, a bike," Ian conceded, smiling. "And then I'm up and running. Or up and cycling, anyway."

"Well," Paul said, drinking from his pint, "you've chosen a good time to come back to Scotland. Whatever your reasons. Things are starting to happen here again."

"In what way?"

"Politically, I mean. There's no doubt there's a major movement towards self-government. It's bound to come – independence, maybe."

For the remainder of their final pints they talked, rapidly and warmly, about Scottish politics as Paul briefed Ian on all that had happened during his absence.

They stepped out into the cold, dry March evening. Their routes took them in opposite directions, and as they paused outside the pub Paul deliberately revived a custom they had had three years ago: he held out his hand for Ian to shake. Ian took it, grinning in obvious awareness that the practice was, by Scottish standards, rather eccentric; and also, Paul suspected, with awareness that it was a socially acceptable substitute for a hug.

He wanted to say, 'I'm glad you're back', but in the circumstances the words would hardly have been sensitive. He contented himself with lingering over their handshake: "Hey," he said, "I'm sure you'll be OK. I'm sure things will work out for you here."

Ian merely nodded, still smiling, before they separated with a wave.

TWO

Paul watched Ian across the crowded room. Although it was a Friday evening he was supposed to be working: they were at the launch of a new book by one of Scotland's best-known writers, and he was there to meet with fellow-publishers, editors, agents, reviewers, and writers – a recognisable literary world, part Glaswegian, part London. But as he stood with his wine-glass in one hand and fiddling with his tie with the other he was hardly listening to the conversation in the small group he had joined.

Ian was present as his guest, though there were several people in the room who had been part of their social circle when they first knew each other. Ian was talking with one of them now, across a small table set against the wall. Whatever they were talking about, it was animating him in a way Paul hadn't witnessed on any of the four occasions they had met since his reappearance in the Carnarvon. He felt that at last he was seeing the Ian he had known three years ago: as if the shadow of his marriage break-up had begun to lift from him and he was again the captivating young man of those days. He had recovered a mannerism from that time which Paul remembered vividly: as he talked his hands were describing shapes in the air, sketching out diagrams of what he was saying. And the person he was talking to was clearly spell-bound by the dancing of his hands, the flow of his words, and – there was no doubt about this – his eyes and his looks. Paul recognised all too clearly in another the effect that Ian could produce on him; he could see the face of Ian's companion – a dark-haired young woman who was an English teacher in Dumbarton.

The voice of one of the people he was supposed to be talking to interrupted him: "I think his new book of short stories is wonderful stuff – as good as anything he's done."

"Really?" Paul said. "I thought they were all totally

predictable. It's the fourth time he's published the same book."

The remark caused obvious offence. Paul didn't care; at that moment he couldn't have cared if the book had been the greatest in the history of Scottish literature. He'd remembered the girl's name: Sonia. Damn Sonia. She had begun leaning across the table, imperceptibly moving closer to Ian. And now he was leaning closer to her. He'd stopped the dancing of his hands; their conversation had evidently moved on to more confidential matters. They laughed together. It was a warm May evening; he was in jeans and a white tee-shirt, so tight that when he stretched as if to hear her better Paul could distinctly see the musculature of his torso. They laughed much more loudly; she briefly drew back, and then closed in on him again. Oh fuck, Paul thought, I can't stand here and watch this.

"You must excuse me while I circulate," he said. The insincerity of his smile was mirrored by the insincerity of the smiles he saw in return; clearly his heretical opinions of the short stories made his departure easy to bear. He crossed to the bar, bought a double whisky, and moved to a corner of the room from where the crowd barred any view of the table against the wall. To his relief he found one of 'his' writers standing there, looking lonely. Talking shop, passing on encouraging news about sales figures, he was able to push other matters out of his mind. The writer drifted off, but a gay man and a lesbian couple came up to join him. The company of 'the tribe' was particularly welcome at that moment, and with the help of another whisky he was soon joining in their instinctively shared humour.

He was considering if he ought not to move on and do some work – he wanted to speak with the Literary Editor of the *Glasgow Herald* – when to his surprise, he saw Sonia leaving. Alone. He lingered where he was, watching the door in case either she returned or Ian followed her. Instead, a few minutes later, he spotted Ian on the other side of the room, standing now with the young editor of a left-wing journal, talking as brightly as before. Noticing

Paul watching him he grinned and raised his glass.

The lesbian couple moved away, leaving Paul with Dave, his gay friend. They continued talking till Dave laughed and changed the subject of their conversation.

"You're after him, aren't you?"

"After who?" But Paul smiled as he said it.

"That blond creature you haven't taken your eyes off for the last quarter of an hour."

Paul laughed loudly and turned so that his back was to Ian: "What blond creature? I don't know who you're talking about."

"Is he to be had?"

Paul felt himself grinning wickedly: "He certainly *was*. But he's a married man now."

"My dear, what difference does that make in Glasgow? They don't call this city the bisexual capital of the world for nothing."

"Well, I'm not sure. He's only recently separated from his wife."

"They don't come any easier. Looking for comfort, and *where* can they find it better than in the arms of a tender loving queen?". Dave started to move away. "I won't cramp your style any longer."

"No, honestly," Paul protested, "there's no need . . ."

But Dave disappeared into the crowd, turning and winking as he did so.

Paul stood slowly finishing his whisky. His eyes went back to 'the blond creature'. He remembered words he'd used to Alex about him: 'it was lust at first sight'. In stark terms Paul recognised what he was feeling now towards Ian: cold, animal lust. He believed he would be reacting the same way if he knew nothing at all about him, if he knew nothing about the attractiveness of his personality or the glamour of his semi-Americanness. It was Ian's body he wanted, and his desire was being fuelled in the most basic way possible. Ian's jeans were very tight. Even across the room Paul could see that his basket was pushed fully to the right side of his crotch; and he was a well-hung man. Paul was not usually so crudely phallocentric, but that bulge below the waist set the final seal for him on the irresistibility of the lean figure in his white tee-shirt and faded denim.

The left-wing editor wandered away from Ian. He was left alone, suddenly seeming lost in the roomful of people of whom he knew so few. Within seconds Paul was by his side. He brightened instantly: "Were you avoiding Ben?" he asked, meaning the editor.

"Ben?" Paul hadn't given him a thought, but now he looked round to see who might be in earshot. "Ben used to be boring, but good-looking. Now he's just boring."

Ian laughed: "Ah, you're a cruel man".

"Am I? Anyway, how are you enjoying yourself?"

"Fine. I've been meeting people I haven't seen for a long time."

"Like Sonia?"

"Yes."

His tone was completely matter-of-fact. Paul spoke more quietly: "I thought you were doing alright there."

Ian looked astonished: "With Sonia?"

"Yes."

He started to laugh: "Nah, not at all. We were just having a friendly discussion. What did you think was happening?"

"Never mind what *I* thought, it's what Sonia thought." Paul lowered his voice still further: "She was doting on you, man."

"Ah, rubbish!" But it was clear he found the suggestion flattering. Paul, in his relief, was able to be amused: "Do you mean to tell me you didn't notice?"

Ian grinned.

"I think you were letting your imagination run away with you."

"Was I hell! You were well in there, I tell you. What were you talking to her about?"

"F R Leavis."

Paul burst out laughing: "F R Leavis? God, no wonder she went home. I'm afraid marriage seems to have dulled your chat-up routines."

Ian shook his head, still grinning.

"I wasn't chatting her up, I tell you."

"I'll believe you. Anyway, what were you saying about Leavis?"

"I was defending him."

"Defending Leavis?"

"Yes."

"You were defending the man who did more harm to English literature than any other single individual in history?"

"Nonsense!"

They began to argue the point. Soon Paul found that, though he easily had the better of the argument intellectually – which was unusual with Ian – it was becoming more and more difficult for him to concentrate on what Ian was saying; sometimes he had to ask him to repeat himself. His attention was constantly being distracted by the animation in Ian's features, the brightness of his eyes, the sexiness of the body now so close to him; he was unaware of anyone else in the room, or even that there were other people in the room; for him Ian and he could have been standing on a desert island, alone in their exchange of wit, the sharing of their erudition, the pleasure of talking almost as a game, a *jeu d'esprit*.

At last he realised that people were starting to leave. He glanced at his watch; it was nine o'clock. The launch had begun at six.

"I don't know about you," he said, "but I'm fucking ravenous."

"Yeah, me too."

"How do you fancy getting a take-away and coming back to the flat? I'm afraid I can't be bothered starting to cook something at this time of night."

"Sounds OK to me!"

"Give me a moment to take my leave of one or two people then, and I'll be with you."

A few minutes later they walked out into the clear May evening and headed towards the city centre. Off Sauchiehall Street they bought an Indian take-away, and were soon in Paul's flat. It was the first time Ian had been there; until now their evenings together had been spent in pubs.

They ate in Paul's lounge. Paul, still in his smart shirt and suit trousers, but glad to be rid of his jacket and tie, opened a bottle of wine.

"Here's looking at you, kid," he said as he raised his glass. The toast was becoming a standing joke between them.

They talked about their respective work. Ian had resumed painting: "It's an odd life," he said. "Very strange after New York."

"In what way?"

"I don't see very many people. I cycle across the city, work alone, cycle back to my room – I mean, my flat-mates are around of course, but I don't have much to do with them. I sit and read, go to bed, get up next morning, cycle off again, spend another day in the studio – and so it goes on."

It sounded a dismal life for a man in his early thirties; and Paul wondered just how much more dismal it must seem to someone who until a few months before had had a marital home in the heart of a great city. But he didn't want to encourage Ian's thoughts in that direction: "After we've eaten I'll give you a guided tour of Casa O'Neill."

Ian looked around him: "It seems a great flat. You've certainly got plenty of space."

There was no overt envy in his tone; but his meaning, escaping perhaps despite himself, was clear. Paul changed the subject: "Talking about painting, have you seen the new exhibition at Third Eye?"

Ian had trenchant opinions about it. Paul was content to listen, knowing that Ian's mind had turned away from New York.

"I'll fix us some coffee," he said when they had finished eating.

In his kitchen, as he waited for the water to boil, he wondered how exactly to proceed next. He had never before in his life attempted to *re*-seduce someone, and he was uncertain of the protocol. To behave as if they hadn't already shared a bed would be ridiculous; nonetheless, that adventure was a long time in the past, and there was no guarantee Ian would appreciate the suggestion that it should be repeated. Paul wasn't so drunk that he didn't know common-sense was against making any move. But it was Friday night and he had a man in his flat he was longing to get the pants off; he had to try something, if only for the sake of his self-respect. The question was, how?

As he went back into the lounge he saw his chance. Ian was standing by his bookshelves, which on one wall ran from floor to ceiling, looking up at the higher shelves. Paul put down their coffees without speaking. As Ian stretched to see the books his jeans were pulled even tighter over his arse; Paul could see he was wearing briefs and not shorts.

He took the two short steps to be behind him and in one impulsive move clasped him round his chest and waist. He felt Ian startle and heard him draw in his breath sharply. For several seconds he stayed tense, on tiptoe. Then, to Paul's relief, he relaxed backwards into the arms which were holding him. Paul lightly kissed the back of Ian's neck, letting his lips do little more than brush the skin below the blond curls: "You're fucking gorgeous," he said quietly. "Do you know that, Ian? You're still as fucking gorgeous as you ever were."

Ian briefly laughed. Paul hugged him tighter; he made no effort to resist. Paul moved closer and now let his lips touch the back of Ian's cheek. Very slightly, but perceptibly, Ian moved his head sideways, so that the touch could become a kiss.

Next morning Ian came into the kitchen as if shyly: he stood just inside the door, barefoot, with an uncertain smile which Paul, looking up from the newspaper laid out on the table, was instantly touched by.

"Well, *you* certainly sleep well," he said, at once making a joke of the situation."I was going to bring you a cup of coffee, but you were still out like a log."

"I'd love a coffee now, though."

"No problem," Paul said, standing up. As he poured it

he asked: "What do you have for breakfast these days?"

"Waffles. "

Paul turned round: "Waffles?"

But Ian was grinning. Paul laughed: "You'll have burnt toast, and like it. Seriously, there's eggs, or porridge, or some Golden Grahams if you're into that kind of thing." He added: "The porridge is the high-risk option."

"Coffee'll do me fine, thanks. I'm not a great breakfast man."

He sat down and pulled over a section of the paper. For some time they sat reading in silence at opposite ends of the table, till Ian looked up and asked: "Just how many rooms have you got in this place?"

"Three, plus kitchen and bathroom. Why do you ask?"

"Oh, only because every time I walk along your hall I lose count of the number of doors."

Paul grinned; he liked the occasions when Ian imitated his own style of humour back to him.

"What's the third room for?" Ian asked.

"The servants. No, it's supposed to be a guest bedroom, but really it's just a lumber room. Let me show you, if you've finished your coffee."

They crossed the hall, and Paul opened the door on to a room he hadn't decorated in the two years he'd been living in the flat. Apart from an unmade single bed by the wall it stored all the possessions he didn't currently need – including his word-processor.

"Originally I intended to take in a tenant," he said, "to raise a little extra cash. But I realised I didn't need the money, and so . . ." His voice became quieter: "To tell you the truth, I've grown used to living alone. I like it. I don't think I could bear to have someone around all the time again."

Ian didn't comment. Paul glanced at him: he was frowning slightly, as if he was trying to understand the sentiments Paul had expressed and not succeeding. Paul closed the door quietly: "Anyway, there you are. Now you've seen round the whole chateau."

Ian turned to him, bright again: "Thanks. Like I said

before, it's a great flat. You're very lucky. Listen – I'd like to have a shower before I go. Is that possible?"

"Of course it is. Come along and I'll get you a towel."

They went into the bedroom, where the curtains were still drawn against the morning sunshine. Paul brought out two towels from a drawer.

"Actually, I haven't had a shower myself yet."

"Oh – do you want to go first?"

Paul turned and grinned.

"That's not what I meant." He glanced down at the unmade bed. "Since we're both going to be taking our clothes off again . . ." He looked at Ian and raised an eyebrow. "It seems a waste to go to all that trouble just for the sake of soap and water."

Ian laughed and looked down at the floor; when he looked up again he very slightly shook his head: "I'm afraid I really need to be going pretty quickly."

Paul's stomach tensed. He made sure no reaction showed as he handed Ian the towel: "OK, no problem."

Ian padded out of the room. Paul heard the bathroom door open and close. He could at least have stripped in here, he thought, suddenly longing to see Ian's body again as the shower started to run. The knowledge that just through the wall Ian was naked was too much for him; he went back to the kitchen and washed up noisily, to drown the sound of the running water to the shower.

When Ian reappeared he was dressed for the street. Paul turned to him, drying his hands, and then saw with surprise that Ian was smiling the same uncertain smile he had had when he came through for breakfast. Paul's confidence jumped as he crossed the room to hug him, and rose still further when Ian, with no apparent hesitation, joined in a lingering mouth-to-mouth kiss. Paul had to break it off; he was hardening fast and he didn't want Ian to feel the pressure against his groin.

"I hope," he said quietly, "you're not regretting last night?"

"No, not a bit."

It was said with an air of such simple candour that Paul

laughed: "There never seems to be any easy way to ask this question - would you like to do the same thing again some time?"

Ian looked away: "That depends."

"On what?"

Ian's eyes came back to meet his: "You know the score, Paul."

Paul nodded slowly.

"Of course I do. I always have." To lighten the mood he made himself joke: "What you mean is, tonight you might meet some gorgeous girl and be swept completely off your feet?"

"I should be so lucky! No, the thing is . . .". He seemed embarrassed again. "I don't want any misunderstandings. I don't want you to think, any time I go out for a drink with you . . ."

"That I should have a packet of condoms handy?" They both laughed. "No," Paul went on, "I take your point. Don't worry." He leaned against the doorjamb: "Look – I have other interests as well, you know." He jerked his head in the direction of the bedroom. "My fun and games. I guess I'm a kind of bisexual too, in my way."

Ian's eyes brightened with surprise: Paul saw that this was a new consideration for him. He went on: "What I'm saying is, monogamy isn't my strong point." He laughed and clasped Ian's shoulder: "Oh dear, one day you'll get used to the gay way of handling relationships."

Ian laughed in his turn: "I don't know about that! What *is* the gay way?"

"Oh, we don't want to get into that debate right now. What I'm asking is, can we be friends who sometimes sleep together?" He rested his hand again on Ian's shoulder: "Because I'd really like that. But no confusion on either side – and no pressure."

Ian nodded.

"Yeah. Yeah, I think that could work."

Paul grinned.

"Of course it could bloody work, you idiot. How do you think I organise my entire life?"

They hugged again, tightly, before Paul unlatched the front door to let Ian out.

"Of course," Alex said, "I would never go back to an old relationship. That's a certain recipe for disaster. Every time."

"Oh, shut up," Paul said. They were in the oddly-named Chimmy Chungas, a large and noisy pub near Alex's bedsit.

"Seriously," Alex went on, "how long do you expect it to last? Three months? Three weeks? Till tomorrow?"

"I don't care how long it lasts."

"Oh, of course you don't! Look, I bet you what you like that the moment he finds a new woman in his life, he'll be off again."

Paul shrugged.

"Probably."

"But that's totally unsatisfactory!"

"Why? Anyway, I'm not so sure he *would* be off. I think he's more genuinely bisexual than I realised."

"What evidence have you got for that?"

"What he got up to in New York."

Alex was immediately interested: "Did you ask him about that?"

"Of course I did! Like you said before, I had to make sure . . . He'd been careful, of course, he's not a fool. But he'd been on the New York gay scene sometimes."

"So *that's* why his marriage broke up?"

Paul shook his head.

"He says, not. He says his wife never knew about it."

"How come?"

"Apparently her job took her out of town quite a bit – upstate, or downriver, or whatever. And sometimes, when she was away . . . Our friend ventured into wicked places."

Alex looked sceptical.

"I bet she *did* know. Somehow. It doesn't seem very likely his marriage breaking up wouldn't have something to do with him being bisexual."

"Well, whatever. Perhaps you're right. The important

thing is, he's in Glasgow now, and much happier than when he first came home. He's really settling in. He's back into painting with gusto, and he's working hard. He's even lost that blasted American accent he sometimes slipped into. And right now" – Paul raised his pint – "I'm happy, too."

"I don't see how you can be. "

Alex's persistence was beginning to irritate Paul: "Why not?"

"Because it won't last!"

"So? You might as well say I can't enjoy this pint" – he raised his glass again – "because in fifteen minutes there'll be nothing left of it. Or that you can't enjoy Beethoven's *Ninth* because you're sitting thinking, 'in an hour's time this'll be over'."

"That's completely different!"

"God, you're just like a heterosexual, do you know that?"

"*Me*?". Alex hooted with laughter: "Do you seriously mean *me*?"

Paul grinned.

"Yes, you. You've got a single model of what a relationship should be, just like straights. The whole point about being gay" – Paul spread his arms to illustrate his point – "is that you're free and flexible about how you work your relationships. One day Ian and me will just be friends again, and nothing more. I can live with that. I enjoy his company as much as I enjoy his body. Well . . . ". He giggled: "Well, nearly as much, anyway. But for the time being I've got both. And while that lasts, I'm going to enjoy it."

Alex didn't reply. Paul couldn't be sure if his arguments had begun to win Alex over, or if Alex was just at last being tactful, and keeping his own counsel.

THREE

Paul and Ian were drinking in the Bon Accord. In the two months since they had resumed their affair it had become a regular venue for the Friday nights they now habitually spent together; they liked it because it served a range of English beers. Paul sipped from a glass of Greene King: "God, I tell you, the very taste of English beer brings back a thousand memories." He raised the glass and grinned. "Well, here's looking –"

"Don't say it!"

"Tell me," Paul asked, "apart from the beer, do you miss anything else about England after all this time? Or are your English years just a distant memory now?"

"Oh, no way – I had some good times in England." Ian smiled. "I won't upset you with the details."

"I see!"

"But what do I miss now? It's an interesting question." He put down his pint and thought about it. "The other main thing is English churches."

"Country churches?"

"Yes. Why so surprised?"

Paul laughed: "Because you're the only other Scot I've ever met who has expressed the slightest interest in English church architecture."

"Ah, rubbish. There must be thousands of us."

"Well, I haven't met any. You've no idea how Steve used to moan when I dragged him round village churches in Sussex. He used to say, 'when you've seen one, you've seen them all'."

"The barbarian!". Ian's voice had the laughter of irony in it.

"Not so much barbarian, as just Scottish, I'm afraid. He had a distinct Presbyterian streak in him, did Steve."

"Nothing worse!"

Their discussion began to roam over English architecture as they compared styles of churches and cathedrals, till they came on to Anglicanism itself, which Ian decried: "As someone said – who was it? I can't remember – 'who can take seriously a church that sprang from the ballocks of Henry VIII?"'

Paul pretended to be shocked: "That's a trifle crude, if I may say so." He reverted to his normal voice: "Oh, come on, Anglicanism has its points."

"Name one."

"Evensong in King's College Chapel, Cambridge, at dusk on a winter's afternoon. Pure magic."

"Pure sentimentality."

"Sentimentality! What do you mean, 'sentimentality'?"

"That's just part of a clichéd image of England. It's got nothing to do with the real England."

"What do you mean, 'the real England'? Are you suggesting that when I sat in King's College Chapel, etcetera, etcetera, I was experiencing an illusion?"

"The illusion is, the context into which you're putting the experience."

Paul tapped the table with his forefinger: "That's just gabble. Explain."

And they were off, into what Paul privately called to himself 'a three-pint argument'. As they got into the rhythm of their talk – energetic, absorbing – Ian resumed the mannerism of moving his hands incessantly to illustrate and emphasise the points he made, shaping his sentences in the air as if his imagination as an artist automatically translated them for him into visual forms. Sometimes this mannerism greatly amused Paul, when he wondered how on earth Ian managed never to send his pint flying off the table; it was as if his finger-tips possessed some secret sense which enabled them to judge the location of a glass of beer to the nearest millimetre.

By the end of the three pints – the last being Theakstons, which because of its strength they had to drink more slowly – they were deep into discussing Eastern Orthodoxy, a subject which intrigued Paul and on which

Ian, who had studied the philosophy of religion as part of his undergraduate course, was well informed. They argued about the *filioque* clause, the insertion into the Nicene Creed which separated the West from Orthodoxy. Paul defended it, not because he believed the Spirit did indeed proceed from the Father 'and the Son', or even cared, but simply because he wanted to hear Ian talking further about Eastern philosophies. Paul often adopted the strategy of arguing a position for its own sake, partly because he enjoyed the intellectual challenge, and partly to act like the grit in the oyster of Ian's intelligence, stimulating him into producing pearls perhaps not of wisdom, but at least of lively and challenging thought.

At last the discussion ran its course. They decided on a whisky to finish this part of the evening; it was Ian's round. While he was waiting at the short, crowded bar, Paul looked round the pub thinking with a conscious surge of pride, 'not only am I with the best-looking man in this pub, I'm with the most intelligent'. Though apart from one thin man in glasses, of about his age, who for some time seemed to have been having a distressing argument with his own male companion, he doubted whether anyone else cared a toss about who might or might not be handsomer than Ian.

Paul's apparently fellow gay man was angrily saying something about America, which reminded Paul of the date. When Ian came back with their whiskies he started to tease him: "I suppose you noticed what day it was yesterday?"

Ian briefly smiled, and looked down.

"Yes." It had been the Fourth of July.

"Did you do anything American, then?" Paul continued, with a mocking sweetness of tone. "Did you carry a gun for the day, or something like that? I noticed the Concert Hall was flying the Stars and Stripes – did you feel an urge to recite the Pledge of Allegiance as you went cycling past?"

Ian looked up. He wasn't smiling: "Cut it, Paul."

Paul was astonished.

"What's up?"

"Cut it. Don't knock America. It's a fine country."

"Bloody hell! I was only joking, Ian. Don't tell me you became a Republican over there as well as an American?"

"That isn't funny, either."

Paul sat back.

"For fuck's sake!" He had often known Ian's moods to change unpredictably, but never as much as this. "What's the matter with you? Have you suddenly lost your sense of humour?"

Ian looked down.

"If you must know, I did do 'something American' yesterday. I got a letter from my wife's attorney."

Oh shit, Paul thought.

"Oh, I'm sorry," he said. "I'm sorry." He defended himself: "But I couldn't have known that, Ian."

Ian didn't reply. When he looked up again he raised his eyebrows, and shrugged. Paul didn't dare ask what the letter's contents were; but he assumed he didn't need to.

He gently changed the subject, talking about a book he had begun to edit which he knew Ian would be interested in. Ian answered politely, and their conversation resumed an apparently smooth course. But Paul suspected that the thoughts of both of them were elsewhere. He wondered if the Fourth of July held some special memory for Ian: perhaps of one particular magic day, one of those days which stand out in any relationship, when he and Mary had stood together watching the fireworks. Perhaps he had even proposed to her on the Fourth of July – it fitted into the timescale of their rapid courtship.

He felt a stab of guilt about the pride he had savoured only a few minutes before. His happiness in this affair depended on the fact that Ian, in a major part of his life, was unhappy. Suddenly he wondered if the affair wasn't both absurd and fragile: a bubble floating on the surface where their two lives had, for the time being, met again. It could burst at any moment; Alex had judged rightly from the beginning.

Their intention had been to go back from the pub to

Paul's flat, as usual. But when they went out into the street Paul stopped on the pavement.

"Listen, Ian" – he couldn't look at him as he asked it – "do you still want to come to the flat?" He made himself bring his eyes round to him. "Because if you'd prefer . . .". But Ian was already smiling, and shaking his head: "Of course I would. Yes."

Paul nodded, trying to show nothing of his relief: "OK."

Their lovemaking was always gentle – almost boyish: the exact opposite of the kind of SM sex which since the start of their affair Paul had discontinued searching for. That night it seemed to him more gentle than ever, and when Ian was asleep beside him – he always fell asleep long before Paul – he lay gazing at the head of blond curls on the pillow. He remembered what Dave had said about separated husbands: 'looking for comfort, my dear'. Surely that was mostly what this strange, once-a-week relationship gave Ian; what he found in this bed.

Paul stretched out and put his arm over Ian's chest. In his sleep Ian gave a quiet grunt of satisfaction and pressed back into the offered embrace. Very softly Paul kissed the back of his head. Well, he thought, if I give you comfort, I've done worse things in my life; and you most certainly give me comfort in return.

About three weeks later, mid-week, he received a phone-call from Tim, a leather and SM contact of his whom he hadn't heard from for some months. They chatted in general terms – Tim, like himself, was a professional man in Glasgow, and their sense of humour was very similar – before Tim brought the subject round to the possibility of their meeting up for a session.

"I'm afraid I can't," Paul said. "Not at the moment."

"Oh?"

Tim's tone made Paul laugh: "There's someone around these days." He explained the circumstances.

"I see," Tim said when he'd finished. "And you don't want to shock him?"

"No," Paul admitted. "But to be honest, I don't think it's

going to be a very long-lasting affair. I'd like to get in touch again sometime – when it's more convenient."

Tim agreed to the arrangement. But afterwards Paul was stirred and restless; that night, for the first time in a long time, he jerked off to a leather fantasy.

On Friday evening, when he and Ian were sitting in his front room with their arms casually round each other's shoulders, Paul said: "There's something I'd like you to do for me."

Ian's head turned: " What?"

"Well – you're virtually the same build as me, aren't you?"

Ian laughed: "I suppose so. Why?"

"I'd like you to try on my leather gear."

Ian laughed more loudly, but shook his head: "No way."

"Whyever not?"

"No way," Ian repeated.

"Just for a bit of fun. I just want to see what you'd look like in it. I want to see if it suits you."

"I certainly hope it wouldn't!"

"I've got nothing else in mind," Paul said quietly. "Just leather."

"If you had," Ian said, "I'd be right out the front door."

Paul had to persist, gently, before he could wear down Ian's resistance to the idea. But at last he persuaded him to change, in the bedroom, into leather trousers and the biker's jacket which Bob had given him in Eassord. He stood in the lounge waiting for Ian to reappear; he had told him to wear nothing but the leather.

When Ian came through the door he was smiling uncertainly. He stopped and looked down at himself.

"I feel completely ridiculous," he said, and looked up again with the same smile.

After a moment Paul said: "Well, you aren't. Believe me, you aren't. Come over here and stand in the light." Ian did so. Paul moved to be closer to him. "Put your head back a little. A little more. Now stand arms akimbo." The light from the table lamp glinted on Ian's bare chest and along the black stretches at his crotch. "Jesus!" Paul exclaimed softly. He had never seen Ian look more sexy. He wondered how to tell him so: "It does suit you," he said quietly, and repeated: "It does suit you."

Ian relaxed the pose and laughed: "I don't think I want to hear that!"

"Stand like you were before," Paul said sharply. "That's it – don't frown, just look natural."

"I've never felt less natural in my life."

Paul simply shook his head. He didn't want to explain to Ian why it was that the image he was presenting was so potent. He wasn't in the least like the stereotype of a leatherman: his curls and slender torso made him look boyish and tender, while the jacket exaggerated his shoulders and the trousers held him tight within their black sheen: he was at once unambiguously masculine and humanly vulnerable; the combination was almost turning Paul aside from awareness of anything except his lust. He cooled himself by joking: "Actually, I might have known this was a mistake. You look far better in my leather gear than I do."

Ian grinned: "Well, I can't help that."

"No, indeed you can't," Paul said wryly. "You know *why* you look better, don't you?" He stepped forward and ran his hand over Ian's crotch. "Let me put it this way – I'm glad I don't ever have to share a public shower with you."

Ian laughed and stepped back: "Ah, why are gay men always so crude?"

"'Gay' men?" Paul exclaimed. "Don't you just mean 'men'?". Ian didn't answer. Paul stepped forward again and this time put his arms round Ian: "Are you telling me you don't enjoy feeling big tits?"

"Not particularly."

Paul ignored the reply. He moved behind Ian and began rubbing his hands over the back of his trousers. They were stretched to smoothness across his arse and tugged forward into the base of his crack; Paul clasped him again and closed his hand round the leather where it was pushed out and down between his legs – but less so than he had either hoped or expected: none of this seemed to be doing anything for Ian. But by now the impetus of his own desire couldn't be held back: "Ian" he said, "I have to have it now. I can't wait. I'm going to rip my Marks and Spencers' best if we don't do something."

Ian twisted his head: "Here?"

He was obviously unenthusiastic. Paul pretended he hadn't noticed: "Yes. That rug in front of the fire is perfectly comfortable - believe me."

Ian didn't dissent. Paul stripped, almost tugging off his things till he was in his Y-fronts: "Lie down," he said.

For a minute he was content, with his hands and tongue, to explore Ian's chest and thighs as if they had never had sex before. Then he said in an urgent whisper: "Take the jacket off and lie on your stomach."

Ian did so, and Paul rid himself of his underpants. He was so close to coming he had only to wank briefly and he was there; as he pushed down against Ian's arse the rub of the leather against his shooting cock made him cry out with pleasure; when it was over he lay sticky and sweating on Ian's back.

Ian said nothing till Paul, recovering his breath, rolled off him. Ian sat up: "Have you got anything to clean us up?" he asked.

His tone startled Paul. He seemed not only not to have enjoyed what had happened, but to have been offended by it. Paul fetched some tissues and dried Ian's back. When he was done Ian said: "I'm going to change."

He padded out of the room. Paul got dressed slowly; all his excitement had faded into a dull, regretful depression. When Ian returned in his shirt and jeans they once again sat side-by-side on the sofa, but no longer with their arms round each other.

"I gather that experiment wasn't a success," Paul said quietly.

"No."

"Well, we won't try it again."

"No, we won't."

Paul turned and looked at him. He was astonished that Ian's manner was still so cold: "What exactly. . ." he began;

after hesitating he resumed: "What was there about it that you – that you disliked so much?"

Ian stared straight ahead.

"I don't like someone having sex with my trousers rather than me."

In another context this sentence might have made Paul laugh out loud; now it made him angry: "That's ridiculous!"

Ian didn't change the direction of his gaze.

"Is it? I don't think so."

"But that's absurd! If I wanted to have sex with my own trousers, all I'd have to do would be to stretch them out on the bed."

"Well, you might as well have done. I was just an accessory after the fact."

Paul sat forward, to look Ian in the face: "That is absolute nonsense."

But Ian persisted: "All I'm saying is, I just felt used. That's all."

"Oh, for God's sake!"

Paul sat back, exasperated with Ian and his moods. He was briefly tempted to accuse him of taking offence wilfully; but decided not to.

They patched up the quarrel before they went to bed. But they didn't have sex, nor in the morning. A faint odour of the row remained in the air over breakfast; but when Ian left at lunchtime they hugged as they always did .

Nonetheless Paul was unsettled. He had begun to wonder if Ian really was at ease with his own sexuality. The previous evening he seemed to have been defining a line beyond which he refused to be drawn into gayness, as if he was saying, 'nothing fetishistic – nothing kinky'. And he also wondered if Ian had reacted against the element of simulated buggery in the experience; he had told Paul before that he disliked the very idea of being penetrated.

Despite the fact that he was the one of them who had had an orgasm in the last twenty-four hours, Paul felt no sense of sexual satisfaction. In the early evening he rang Tim and asked if it was possible to change his mind about meeting up; was Tim free the following afternoon? He was.

Ian rang him at work on Thursday: "Usual arrangement for tomorrow?" he asked cheerfully. It was clear that the previous weekend's quarrel was either forgotten or forgiven.

But Paul hesitated.

"Eh . . . yes, I suppose so. The Bon Accord abut nine?"

"Suits me."

"See you then, then. "

They were finishing their third pints before Paul found the courage to say to Ian: "Look, I don't want you to misunderstand this, but . . . I'm not entirely sure it would be a good idea for you to come back tonight. I mean, assuming you want to."

Ian's look expressed his surprise. Paul went on quickly: "It's got nothing to do with last week – well, it has sort of, but not with you." He lowered his voice: "Look, I can't really talk about it here. Why don't we go on to the Griffin, and I'll explain on the way?"

Ian raised his eyebrows: "I'm agog!" he said, and drained his pint.

As they crossed the motorway Paul told him about Sunday: "You see, Tim is really into quite heavy SM – at least, by my standards – and we spent quite a bit of time together. I mean, we weren't at it non-stop, of course – we kept having breaks and starting again – but . . . it all added up."

To Paul's surprise Ian was grinning.

"What you're trying to tell me," he said, "is that you're still black and blue."

"Heavens, no!" Paul exclaimed. "Well, not as bad as that. Sort of . . .". Even though they were in the street he lowered his voice: "The marks are still visible, yes. Nothing lurid, but . . . visible," he repeated.

"So where's the problem?"

God, Paul thought, will I ever be able to predict how this man's going to react to anything?

"The problem is, I'd rather you didn't see me like that."
"Well, you can always wear pyjamas."
Paul stopped.
"Look, Ian, I'm perfectly serious. I'd rather you didn't come back tonight."
Ian shrugged.
"OK. If you feel so strongly about it. But I think you're being a bit hyper-sensitive."
"All the same," Paul insisted.
As they resumed walking he said: "We'll make up for it next week. Let's do something special – have a day out somewhere, for example."
In the pub they agreed where it would be: "Edinburgh," Paul said. "But on one strict condition."
"Which is?"
"We do nothing cultural whatsoever." The Edinburgh Festival was about to start. Ian laughed: "No culture?"
"Absolutely not. I'll have enough of that during the week, when I'm through for the Book Festival. On Saturday we'll just be mindless tourists."
Ian laughed again.
"If that's what you want!"

They went through by train:
"I'm not taking the car," Paul said, "to drink low-alcohol lager in the city with the best pubs outside London."
Even before they left the flat Paul had a sense that this was going to be an extraordinary day. The previous evening Ian had been in his most attractive humour – joking, grinning, talking with a vivacity which reminded Paul why, four years previously, he had found him irresistible. When he was in this mood Ian's features became transformed as if from within: he wasn't merely handsome, he was charismatic.
There was a good reason for Ian's humour. He had been accepted to take part in a major exhibition in the city later in the year and was no longer working merely for his own pleasure, or for the sake of it; he had a specific goal in mind, and the prospect seemed to have galvanised him.

Paul was astonished by the hours he was putting in: twelve hours a day, in his bare little studio in Dennistoun. The effects showed; they went to bed early, and after sex Ian was immediately asleep. Soon Paul got up again and sat reading for two or three hours before he rejoined Ian. This difference in their sleeping patterns was one of the few ways in which he was conscious of the age-gap between them; since his late thirties he had needed less and less sleep.

In Edinburgh they wandered about, as Paul had suggested, like tourists. They went into the Castle, and amongst the restless, multi-lingual crowd in the tiny Crown Room they admired the Scottish Regalia. It was one of the few moments of the day when their mood was serious: "Will we *ever* be independent again?" Paul asked, half to himself, as the visitors glanced at the simple, ancient Crown and immediately passed on.

"Of course we will!" Ian said. "No doubt at all."

Paul shook his head: "Christ, I wish I shared your confidence."

They headed towards the exit on to the turnpike stair: "If I didn't think Scotland was one day going to be independent, I wouldn't stay," Ian said.

Paul pondered this as he started to descend the narrow staircase.

"I think you're right," he remarked over his shoulder. "I don't think I would either."

Outside, on the ramparts and again on the Esplanade, they took photographs of each other with Paul's camera. As they walked back into the Lawnmarket a note of hilarity seemed to enter Ian's mood: he insisted on going into one gift shop after another, gleefully holding up for Paul's inspection ever more horrible examples of tartan kitsch till they began to attract dirty looks from shopkeepers and puzzled glances from other browsers. At last Paul persuaded him to stop this – "spoilsport," he complained – and they descended to the Cowgate, where they went into Bannermans, a large cavern-like pub, for lunch.

While they were waiting for their orders Ian picked up

one of the tens of thousands of handbills with which the Festival city was strewn: "Are you sure you don't want to do anything cultural?" he asked. "Just as a token?"

"What have you got there?". Ian held it up. "Strindberg?" Paul exclaimed in horror.

"What's wrong with that? I rather fancy the idea of *Miss Julie*."

"Look, I told you – strictly no culture." Paul glanced round the pub and lowered his voice almost to a whisper: "We'll leave that to all these dreadful undergraduates."

"Ah, you're becoming a cantankerous old man!"

Paul nodded: "There's some truth in that. When I was a student I loved the Festival – which reminds me, I was thinking of something the other day."

"Which was?"

"If I'd decided to go into teaching when I graduated, and done a year's training, I'd have been twenty-two when I became a teacher."

"So?"

Paul started to smile.

"You would only have been thirteen. If I'd got a job at your school, I could have been your English teacher."

Ian smiled in turn: "I'd never thought of that."

"Do you realise that means I could have belted you?"

Ian guffawed loudly; when he recovered he said: "You'd have enjoyed that, wouldn't you?"

"It could still be arranged," Paul said slyly.

Ian, though he was still smiling, shook his head firmly: "I don't think so."

"Coward."

Over their pints they began to reminisce about their childhoods. Though Ian grew up in East Kilbride, a new town in the west of Scotland, and Paul in a village in central Scotland, they were both working-class children who had become middle-class adults; and, not for the first time, Paul wondered if this was one of the reasons why they were instinctively drawn to each other – why, so often, they understood each other's jokes without having to spell them out, or reacted in the same way politically, or had a shared sense of intellectual excitement when they debated around an issue: as if, even yet, neither of them had quite lost the sense of discovering new worlds through reading and thought.

Their conversation moved on to their student years – a decade apart, but spent in this city – and after lunch, as they wandered along Chambers Street and the George IV Bridge, they swapped memories of lectures and exam nerves and student pranks. Paul was exploring whole new areas of Ian's life; they had never before talked like this at length.

In Victoria Street they went into a second-hand bookshop to browse. But after a couple of minutes Ian asked: "Are you going to be long?"

Paul turned to him in surprise.

"Not very. Why?"

"It's just that I want to pop down the road – I'll be back in about ten minutes. Will you still be here?"

"Yes, I suppose so." Paul started to smile. "What are you up to?"

"Nothing! I'll see you." And he went off, grinning.

When he came back he was equally mysterious.

"What *are* you up to?" Paul asked again.

"Nothing at all! Have you found anything you're interested in?"

"Only a Foulis Press edition I can't afford – I wish you'd tell me what you've been doing."

Ian had the air of a schoolboy organising a prank: "I've told you – nothing at all!"

It wasn't until early evening, when they were in a tiny, crowded restaurant near Bruntsfield Links which Paul was particularly fond of, that Ian revealed where he had been. After they had placed their orders, and were sampling a fine Burgundy, he suddenly said: "I've got a present for you."

"A present?"

Ian had his mischievous grin again.

"Yes, and one for myself. Hang on a moment."

He dipped into the pocket of his donkey-jacket. A

moment later he placed on the table two small plastic cubes, their faces each about two centimetres square; inside them, resting on a piece of blue cloth, was what looked like a fragment of dark ivory.

"Well!" Paul exclaimed. "That's very kind of you." He looked closely at the cubes. "What exactly are they?"

"Dinosaurs' teeth."

Paul thought he had misheard: "Pardon?"

"Dinosaurs' teeth – I got them from a shop in the Grassmarket."

Paul sat back. He had an impulse to hoot with laughter; but instead he said deadpan: "That is the single most improbable sentence I have ever heard."

Ian burst out laughing: "Why?"

"Do you mean to tell me there's a dinosaurs' teeth shop in the Grassmarket?"

"There's a fossil shop – I went looking for a couple of nice fossils. But instead, I got these." He picked up one of the cubes. "Do you realise this tooth is at least sixty-five million years old?"

"Well, I never," Paul said. "Good Heavens. Is that a fact?"

"Stop being sarky! Aren't you impressed? Just think of it – sixty-five million years!"

Paul looked at him. His eyes had such a childlike quality of wonder Paul started to laugh; but at the same time he realised that for Ian the age of the fossilised tooth was more than just an intellectual fact – it was a reality of which he seemed to have almost a sensory apprehension; as if, defying Eliot, an idea was still for him an experience. Paul, as so often, chose to express his feelings through humour: "You remind me of my nephew, do you know that? This is the sort of thing *he* would go nuts about."

"So?"

"But he's eight years old! And you're thirty-two – allegedly."

Ian was grinning. He repeated: "So? What's wrong with having the same reactions as an eight-year-old – if an eight-year-old is right? We shouldn't let ourselves 'grow up' like that. We 'grow up' far too much – we should stay much more childish than we do. Play much more, for example."

He seemed almost to be inviting Paul to respond satirically. But this time Paul didn't; he said quietly: "Is that what makes you an artist?"

Ian was visibly surprised. He looked down, and for a moment Paul thought he was blushing.

"Oh, I don't think so."

He raised his eyes. Paul remained serious: "I'm not so sure. Maybe that's why you create art, and I merely edit it."

Ian was now unmistakeably discomfited.

"Ah, mince."

"Is it?". Paul picked up the cube nearest to him: "Many thanks for the present, though. But do you mind if I ask – was it expensive?"

Ian shook his head.

"No, not at all."

Paul began to smile again.

"Do you mean to tell me the world is littered with dinosaurs' teeth?"

"Apparently!"

At that moment the waiter interrupted them, with their first course.

After dinner they drank in Bennetts Bar, another of the ornate Victorian pubs for which they shared a taste, and, while it was still daylight, strolled down to Haymarket to pick up the Glasgow train. During the fifty-minute journey they fell quiet, breaking a flow of conversation which had run almost non-stop since breakfast. But when they came to the point in the journey from which they could glimpse Eassord Castle in the distance Paul pointed it out.

"My *heimat*," he said quietly. "Even yet."

From Queen Street station it was just a few minutes walk to Paul's flat. Ian almost literally fell into an armchair: "Christ, I'm knackered!" he exclaimed. "Maybe we overdid it a bit."

Paul went over to the CD player: "Ach, the younger generation of today have no stamina." He selected a disk and looked round: "I'll get us some coffee in a minute.

Meanwhile here's some soothing music for you to listen to while you recover."

"What is it?" Ian asked as it started playing.

"Don't you recognise it?". Paul grinned. "It contains your tune."

"'My' tune?"

"It's Elgar – the *Enigma Variations*."

"Ah! But I still don't get the joke."

"I'll explain when I come back. You do want coffee, I take it?"

Paul was some time in the kitchen. When he re-entered the lounge with their coffees the music was close to the variation he intended to point out to Ian; but Ian, his head lying back against the armchair, was fast asleep.

Paul smiled.

"So much for Elgar," he said softly, and sat on the sofa facing him.

He lifted his own coffee cup, looked at Ian sleeping in the light of a lamp behind his chair, and stopped in mid-movement. For several seconds he sat immobile before, his hand trembling, he put the cup down again as quietly as he could.

The music grew gentle and slow as it approached the opening of what Paul had described as 'your tune', punning on Ian's surname: Nimrod – the Hunter.

The almost indecently moving melody started to fill the room. But Paul was barely conscious of it – not, at least, as a discrete part of what he was experiencing: the music was his emotions, his emotions were the music. A wave of tenderness for Ian had swept through him when he saw him in the lamplight: so intense that now he sat helpless in its power. At the crescendo in the variation Ian stirred and turned his head; Paul was terrified he was going to wake and destroy the moment; but with the sigh of a man deeply asleep from physical tiredness he settled again, with the light falling across his profile.

The music moved on, but Paul sat as he had been before. His mental tumult prevented physical action; all his energies were concentrated on understanding what was happening to him. But naming his emotion was hardly difficult. Only with one man before in his life had he known this feeling, and that was Steve; and he believed not even Steve had ever seemed so beautiful to him as Ian did now. He longed to run his hand slowly through Ian's curls, stroke his cheek, feel the softness of his skin where the suntan of his neck was heightened by the contrast with his white tee-shirt: but he was afraid even to stir in case he woke him.

He sat till the music ended and the CD clicked into silence. Then, moving as if automatically, he stood up and went to the player. He selected the only piece of music which seemed possible in the supercharged state of his emotions: the final movement of Mahler's *Third*.

Ian slept on, in dreamless stillness. Paul sat down again opposite him as strings began to play the calm, rich, seductive Adagio. Paul knew well the title Mahler had given this music: 'what Love tells me'.

How long had he been in love with Ian? Only since today? Since they had first slept together after his return? Since he reappeared so startlingly in the Carnarvon? Or had he gone for four years without once admitting to himself what happened on that October night when they first met? Was it possible that because he didn't believe in any such thing, he had known love at first sight and never realised it?

Whatever the truth of the past, there was no mistaking the truth of the present. He was helplessly, totally in love with Ian. He loved everything about him: the slight crookedness of his nose, the result of breaking it when playing Rugby as a schoolboy; the thickening of his chin which showed how, in a few years time, he would acquire the double chin of middle age; his long, slender fingers, stained here and there with paint; the fall of his tee-shirt across his chest, the fullness of his crotch, the slimness of his thighs.

How could he have hidden from himself for so long the real nature of his feelings? But already he could hear Alex's voice, and other voices, including his own, telling him he was crazy. To fall in love with a married man! What could be crazier? There was no possibility of Ian ever committing himself to a gay relationship; any day he might meet a woman who would re-fire his heterosexuality, and once that side of his sexuality was aflame again it would devour into ashes any relationship between himself and Paul.

This was bound to end badly. What time and chance had given him, time and chance would take away – perhaps tomorrow, perhaps next week, certainly soon. But Paul realised he had no choice but to live through whatever was coming; there was no option for him of withdrawal or self-protection. Now that he understood the truth of how he felt he knew he could no more not love Ian than he could not breathe.

And for the moment, as Mahler's recurrent melody played softly and slowly, he could only be grateful that he had been given this hour of perfection. If only time might stop now, he thought, and never move again: if only this could endure forever, this that I have in the summer evening: the music and the lamplight and Ian's untroubled beauty.

FOUR

The end, when it came, was far more brutal than he had consciously foreseen; though afterwards he believed he had had a premonition of it, on the last night of a short stay, partly a working trip and partly a holiday, in Amsterdam. He had been drinking amongst the leathermen in the Argos bar, savouring the ambience and watching the ritual of passing in and out of the backroom – tonight he had had no inclination to go in himself, but stood with his beer, in leather and denim rather than full leather, relaxing amongst this multi-national tribe-within-a-tribe to which he was happy to belong by virtue of his fetishism. He left the bar just after two 2 am and walked across the city towards his hotel. It was a mild, calm October night.

His hotel was in a street off the Prinsengracht. But when he reached it he wasn't tired, and instead of going indoors he turned back and started to walk slowly by the canal. Eventually he stopped on a bridge and leaned against the rail, looking down on the lights reflected across the rippling water.

He didn't want to go home. It wasn't the normal end-of-holiday feeling – he had only been in the city for five days, and two of those he had spent working – but a much deeper reluctance: almost a bodily dread of returning to the offshore islands, 'the West European archipelago' as Irish nationalists called it. It was approaching the end of October; all the long dark dreichness of a Scottish winter stretched in front of him.

He could hardly bear it. He didn't want to leave the continent; all his instincts were to remain on the landmass and not take flight from it, literally, in a few hours time. It wasn't so much that he wanted to stay on in Amsterdam; it was rather that he longed to go exactly in the opposite direction from the one he was obliged to take – to go south and east, as far away from frost and fog as he could get.

The feeling recurred, less intense, as he sat waiting at Schiphol airport. This time he asked himself how much it had to do with Ian.

He couldn't pretend to himself that the affair was making him happy. He had become far too emotional about Ian, and as a result the relationship was now grotesquely one-sided. He had done his best to conceal from Ian that he was in love with him, rather than merely fond of him, but he wasn't at all certain he'd succeeded; lately there had been occasions when he thought Ian was acting deliberately coolly, as if he was trying to open up a distance between them.

But the trouble was, he couldn't be sure he wasn't imagining this. His fear of losing Ian had begun to burst out unpredictably as a raging jealousy, particularly of any intrusion on their regular times together at the beginning of each weekend. He bitterly resented Ian going to an exhibition opening on a Friday evening – other evenings didn't worry him, but Friday evenings were *their* evenings. The worst incident had been when Ian failed to come on to the flat, as he had promised to do, after an opening at the Collins Gallery. Paul lay awake till five in the morning, his stomach churning and his whole body tense as he thought of what he was sure was happening: of course he'd met a woman, of course this was it, of course he'd made his return to heterosexuality.

The following morning his doorbell rang. When he answered it he found a very hung-over Ian on his doorstep. He'd gone on from the Collins to a party in Hillhead, got roaring drunk, and ended up sleeping on the floor.

Or had he? The jealousy was soon alive in Paul again: was this a plausible story about a man of thirty-two? No-one else involved there somewhere?

No, the affair with Ian didn't give him happiness: but it gave him terror and joy. The hours he spent with Ian were the brightest, the most brilliant he had known since his early days with Steve. As he waited for his flight to be called he deliberately cheered himself by remembering the weekend before last, when they had sat all Saturday afternoon in the Scotia Bar, drinking slowly in the mellow atmosphere of smoke and music. An Irish folk band were playing; it was music Paul loved with such intensity it made him wonder if there really might be such a thing as ancestral memory. As the dazzling fiddlers played he became proud of his surname: was he not, after all, of the great Ulster house of the Uí Néill?

"This reminds me of Dublin," he remarked to Ian.

"Ah!"

"Have you ever been to Dublin?"

Ian shook his head.

"Then I must take you there," Paul said at once. "We'll go over some weekend. After your show – it'll be a pleasant time of the year to be there." The exhibition Ian was participating in had been postponed till February.

"Good idea!"

"Yes," Paul said, stretching out his legs beneath the table. "I tell you, boy, you don't know what a pub is till you've been to Dublin. We'll do all the James Joyce kick. We'll have afternoon tea in Bewley's. And we'll see the Book of Kells in Trinity – I suspect you'll like that."

Ian laughed: "I think I might! Yes, a weekend in Dublin is a definite."

At the end of the afternoon they walked the short distance to the Transmission Gallery, where there was yet another of the openings which punctuated Ian's social life. Paul didn't normally accompany him, since he knew so few of the artists at them, but today he went along and got involved in conversation with one or two people he recognised who straddled the literary and the art worlds in Glasgow. He left Ian there; but before he did so he stood for a few minutes near the door watching him moving about the crowd, laughing and talking with his usual animation – the hand gestures limited on this occasion to the hand which wasn't holding a wine-glass – and looking totally in his natural milieu. He's come home, Paul thought, more completely than I have ever been able to do; and the idea comforted him, that at least of the two of them

Ian was happy. The he slipped quietly out into the October evening.

When he got back to the flat after his flight from Amsterdam there were only three messages on his answering machine. He slept, showered, and ate before he listened to them. The first was from a friend inviting him to dinner; the second from his secretary, about a work matter; and the third from Ian. Before it had stopped playing he had picked up the phone and was dialling Ian's number .

Three days later, on Saturday afternoon, he was sitting in Alex's bedsit.

"So," Alex said after a long silence between them.

"Quite."

"When is she coming over?"

"A week today."

"How long for?"

"Four weeks."

"Good God – hasn't she got a job over there?"

"Yes. But according to Ian her employers have given her a special furlough – whatever that may be," Paul added sarcastically. For three days he had been filled with a bitter hatred of everything American.

"They must be serious, then?"

Paul sat back in the armchair: "Oh, there's no doubt about that. He's going to go back to her, I'm sure of it. I mean, in theory she's coming over to see if they can patch things up – have a trial reconciliation, as it were. But you don't fly the Atlantic on an off-chance."

"Is that what he told you when you saw him?"

"But I haven't seen him! I had a long phone conversation with him on Wednesday, and that's that. He was too busy to come out for a drink, and he's too busy to come out between now and when that" – Paul checked himself. "When she comes," he said. He couldn't bring himself to speak Mary's name.

Alex was, as Paul had known he would be – which was why he had come to see him – sympathetic but not indulgent: "But Paul, you always knew it had no future."

"But I never thought it would end like this!". Paul heard the bitterness in his own voice. "I mean, I always imagined we'd go on being friends – you know yourself how gay relationships turn into friendships, nine times out of ten." Alex nodded slowly. "I thought I'd always have his company at least – the evenings in the pub – the long arguments about anything and everything – maybe even see him one day with a baby on his knee." He had to make a conscious effort to calm himself. "This is the one thing I didn't foresee. That he'd go back to America."

They were quiet again for a while; then Alex said: "It might not work out, though. They might find they can't patch things up."

Paul shrugged.

"Possibly. But I doubt it."

Alex tried a joke: "You could always pop round some day and introduce yourself."

Paul didn't laugh. He said quietly: "He's already told her about all that. "

"*What*? "

"Well, as he himself said" – for the first time in the afternoon Paul smiled – "there wouldn't have been a great deal of point in him bringing her all the way to Glasgow just to sit her down and say, 'Darling, there's something you ought to know'. So he's already told her. Apparently they've been spending hours and hours on the phone, ever since he got her letter."

"And what was her reaction?"

Paul smiled again.

"Can't you guess?"

"She was furious?"

Paul shook his head.

"No. She already knew. Or had sussed it out, anyway. I don't suppose any woman could be that clueless about her own husband – a New Yorker, least of all."

"But surely that changes everything?"

"Of course it does. It makes the marriage a lot more secure. Think about it."

"But does she accept it?"

"She doesn't really need to. He's decided he's going to be faithful to her from now on – he says, if he gets her back he's not going to do anything again to endanger the marriage. Ever."

After a moment Alex said quietly: "He really is in love with her, isn't he?"

"Oh, yes," Paul snapped, suddenly angry with the whole situation – with himself perhaps most of all. "He loves her, alright. If you think about it, he's always been faithful to her."

"How?"

"Well, doesn't it strike you as odd that since he came back to Scotland he's never once made any effort to get involved with a *woman*?"

"Ah!" Alex exclaimed.

"Exactly. He has been faithful to her, in his fashion." All his bitterness rose to the surface: "I was never anything more to him than a convenient sexual release."

For the first time in the conversation Alex showed some impatience: "Now you're just being stupid, Paul."

Paul made no effort to contact Ian again before Mary arrived, or during the first two weeks of her stay. He knew he had no right to intervene: all he could do now was wait on events.

He hoped it would be Ian who would ring him; that there would be an invitation to meet Mary. He prepared himself mentally for this: he'd be civilised, he'd be polite, he'd be thoroughly British. 'Awfully nice to meet you. What do you make of our weather?' .

Then one afternoon he met Mark, a friend of Ian's and another artist, in Sauchiehall Street.

"He's behaving very oddly," Mark said when, as was inevitable, the conversation came round to Ian.

Paul was startled: "In what way?"

"Well, I went round to his flat the other day, to see Elaine" – one of Ian's flatmates – "and Ian and Mary were there, in his room."

"And?"

"Well, they didn't come out of the room. I could hear them moving about and talking, but they never opened the door. I was reduced to saying very loudly in the hall, 'When you see Ian, give him my regards'. It was farcical."

"What's he playing at?" Paul exclaimed in astonishment.

"God knows. I thought I must have done something to offend him, but then Elaine told me he hardly ever leaves his room. Apparently they sit in there all day long – his flatmates have barely seen Mary at all."

"But don't you run into him in Dennistoun?". Mark had a studio in the same building as Ian. He shook his head: "He hasn't been in for about a month."

"You mean he's stopped painting? What about that exhibition he's preparing for?"

Mark shrugged. He would be showing work then himself: "Well, it isn't till February. He's still got plenty of time."

Two days later Paul had a phone-call from another friend of Ian's, one of the crowd they had known when they first met four years previously: "I ran into him yesterday," John said. "In Argyle Street."

"Really? That's the first sighting there's been for ages," Paul remarked sarcastically. "Was he on his own?"

"Yes. I must say, he didn't look very well."

Paul was instantly alert: "How?"

"He looked pale, and quite harassed. Didn't have much to say for himself at all – not like our Ian, that, is it?" John added with a laugh. "I don't suppose we spoke for more than about a minute. To tell you the truth, I got the feeling he was giving me the brush-off. I don't know what I've done to offend him."

"I wouldn't worry," Paul said at once. "He seems to be behaving like that with everybody."

He sat up till the small hours of the morning, drinking whisky and listening over and over again to the Vivaldi *Gloria*. All his thoughts were variations on the one theme: it isn't working out, it's going wrong, he won't be leaving. He won't be leaving.

That Friday evening Paul attended the launch of two of his firm's books, in a small hall hired for the occasion. To all intents and purposes it was a working evening for him; but at one point he took the chance to join Alex and relax from business for a few minutes. He was talking about the possibility of going on later to a gay bar when, in mid-sentence, he stopped.

"What's up?" Alex asked.

It was some moments before Paul could speak: "Turn round slowly," he said, "and look at the couple who've just walked through the door. Over there by the drinks."

Alex did so as if casually; when he turned back he asked: "Who are they?"

Paul was still having difficulty speaking.

"Don't you recognise him from my description? Those blond curls?"

Alex gawped and looked round again, this time much more obviously: "And the woman?" he asked.

"I haven't seen her before," Paul said. "I can only guess who she is." Suddenly he was furious: "How the hell did *they* get an invite? I certainly never asked them".

He couldn't avoid going back to work, mixing with reviewers and writers, but he was scarcely conscious of anything he was saying or doing. All his attention was on the couple who were all too evidently very happy in each other's company; from time to time Ian would put his arm round Mary and give her a short squeeze. She was shorter even than he was, petite and dark, and – Paul hated her for it – very pretty. Damn you, he thought, why couldn't you be fat and ugly? Even across the room he could see that her most striking feature was her eyes: large and brilliant and captivating.

But when at last he joined them, having given himself time to calm down, those eyes were turned on him with what he was sure was mocking amusement as Ian introduced them – without, Paul noticed, the slightest hint of embarrassment.

"Delighted to meet you," Paul said as he shook Mary's hand. He wondered if he had ever said anything less truthful in his life. He turned to Ian: "So, how's things?"

"Fine. OK."

Paul waited for him to go on. When he realised Ian wasn't going to say anything more he turned back to Mary: "How much longer of your holiday have you got to go?"

"A week," she answered, in a strong New York drawl.

"I hope you've enjoyed your stay, anyway."

The mockery in her eyes intensified.

"Oh yes," she said, and laughed.

Paul doubted that he could be successfully hiding his feelings. He looked at Ian again. His eyes were averted; he seemed to be pretending he was much more interested in what was happening on the other side of the room. Paul felt his throat constrict with anger.

"So, what are your plans, then?" he asked.

Ian looked at him and smiled.

"Guess."

The single word enraged Paul. It was several seconds before he could say icily: "You're going back to America, then?"

"Soon as can be arranged."

Mary cut in: "Fortunately, it really isn't very difficult. Nearly all Ian's stuff" – she patted his arm as she spoke his name – "is still in store, in Brooklyn. When I get home next week the first thing I'm gonna do is get it back out again and into our apartment. It'll help fill up all the empty spaces" – they both laughed.

What are these two like? Paul thought. Have they just been playing at being a separated couple?

"You'll be staying on for your exhibition, though, I take it?"

Ian looked momentarily uncertain.

"I don't know. I suppose so."

"You *suppose* so?" The exclamation had escaped Paul before he could check himself.

"Very probably," Ian said quickly.

Paul nodded.

"Good. Good. So there'll be plenty of time to meet up again before you go, then?"

Ian briefly looked down; when he raised his eyes, for the first time in the conversation Paul saw something of the friendliness he had seen in them so many times in the past: "Yes, sure." After a moment he added: "For certain."

The words eased Paul's anger. He smiled: "We'll have to give you a good Glaswegian send-off." He turned back to Mary: "I'm afraid I have to circulate again." He held out his hand; as Mary took it he said: "I hope you have a nice flight back."

He turned away and crossed the room to rejoin Alex.

"Jesus, that was hard work!" he exclaimed.

"Did they say why they'd come?"

"No, but I can guess. I imagine that cow was curious to meet me."

Alex laughed: "Now, now."

"Either that, or they just wanted to rub my nose in it. As soon as this crap's over we're going on to Squires. I need all the alcohol I can get. Just look at them smarming over each other" – but when he turned round, they were gone.

In Squires, the city's principal gar bar, Alex chided him: "There's no point in being bitter, Paul."

"Who's bitter?"

"You are. I mean, come on, you can hardly blame a man for going back to his own wife."

"Are you deliberately trying to sound like Patience Strong?"

Alex laughed: "'Oh, I'm not bitter'", he parodied Paul. "'I'm not bitter all.'" Despite his irritation Paul smiled. "And let's face it – if *you* had the choice between Glasgow and New York, would *you* choose Glasgow?"

"Right now I'd choose any fucking place but Glasgow."

"To tell you the truth," Alex said, "I'm dead envious. Imagine living in New York! I'd love it."

"Oh, God! Why don't you go and seduce Mary Hunter while you've still got the chance? Then *you* can marry her and live in Manhattan, and I'll keep Ian."

On the Monday morning his boss asked him into his office.

"Paul – you remember that Amsterdam job that was

being discussed about this time last year?"

"Yes, I do."

"Well, it's back on the cards again. You still interested?"

"Oh, Christ!" Paul exclaimed. "Not again?"

Derek looked surprised.

"You're *not* interested?"

Paul leaned forward and tapped the desk: "I'm not interested in being fucked around again. How definite is this 'on-the-cards'?"

"Very definite. Much more definite than last year."

Paul leaned back.

"And what are my chances?"

Derek smiled.

"Very good. What did you say to the Dutch when you were over there in October?"

"Not a lot. I spent most of my time chatting up that rep who'd come up from Paris."

Derek laughed.

"Well, maybe your French impressed them, then. Whatever – this is looking much more real than it did last year. They want an English-language editor, willing to be based in Holland for at least two years, possible extension of the contract for another year, and with at least one other European language."

For some seconds Paul gazed steadily at Derek.

"Of course I'm interested," he said quietly. "Very interested."

"Good. I think things might move much more quickly this time."

"How quickly?"

"We might have a firm idea early in the New Year."

Paul burst out laughing: "Is that the Dutch idea of 'moving quickly'?"

Derek looked tolerant rather than amused.

"Be patient, Paul. Remember it takes time to fix up an international contract – even in the single market." Now he smiled. "Or do I mean, '*particularly* in the single market'?"

"Oh, not you as well?" Alex exclaimed when Paul told him.

"Not me as well what?"

"Leaving Glasgow! Is it this year's fashion?"

Paul smiled wickedly.

"Well, if *you* had the choice between Glasgow and Amsterdam, would *you* choose to stay in Glasgow?"

"Not for ten seconds."

"Well, there you are then." Paul became more serious: "I couldn't possibly turn up a chance like this. Even if I wanted to. Which I don't."

Alex studied him. After a moment he asked: "Would you have said the same thing if Blondie wasn't leaving town?"

Paul had anticipated the question.

"Yes. Yes, I would. Though obviously I'd have had mixed feelings about it. But – it would have been a nice ending, at least. And I wouldn't have been that much separated from him – I expect to be back in Glasgow maybe half-a-dozen times a year." He paused, and went on more quietly: "There wouldn't have been the Atlantic Ocean between us. New York just seems so fucking far away."

Alex's tone was brisk: "So if you think about it, in the end everything's working out for the best."

"I wouldn't say that, exactly. Though there's certainly a neat symmetry to it all – I leave for old Amsterdam, and he leaves for New Amsterdam. Probably at about the same time, moreover."

"Yes, and what a pair of good Scots you make, too."

Paul smiled.

"What are you on about now?"

"Well, one of you leaves Scotland the moment he gets back with his wife, and the other leaves the moment he's offered a new job. Call yourself a Scottish nationalist?"

"Well, I'll just have to become a Dutch nationalist," Paul said wryly.

Afterwards he wondered if Alex had realised how much he had been lying. He had thought very carefully about whether he would have applied for the Amsterdam posting if Ian had been staying on in Glasgow; and he knew he wouldn't. To have willingly brought about such a separation, however lightly he spoke of it to Alex, would have been beyond him.

And the impending separation weighed more and more on his spirits as December closed in. Events had been moving with bewildering speed; there had been little more than a month between his return from Holland and Ian's confirmation that he was returning to America. Paul realised he had been almost in a state of shock; now that it was wearing off he was beginning to feel the pain of what he couldn't regard as anything other than a grotesque twist of fate at his expense – the tearing-away from him of the man who had given him the happiest days he had known since he came back to Scotland.

He *was* bitter. Alex was right: but Paul saw no reason why he shouldn't be. Hadn't there been enough suffering in his life already? Hadn't he shed enough tears over the years, that he had to shed more now? Not that he did cry: he drank. He got through bottle after bottle of whisky, alone in his flat.

His longing for Ian's body was a madness which only drunkenness could temper, by dulling every sensation. He longed to see him again; but he wanted it to be Ian who contacted him, not the other way round. He hoped that after Mary's departure Ian would ring him and they could at least go out again for an evening: to sit in the Horseshoe or the Scotia or the Vicky Bar as they had done so many times, talking away the hours over their pints of eighty. But Ian didn't ring.

At last Paul's loneliness got the better of his pride. He dialled Ian's number; a flatmate answered: "I'm afraid he's out."

"Do you know when he'll be back?"

"Sorry, no idea."

"OK. I'll try again tomorrow."

But the next evening the answer was the same. And the night after that. And the night after that. By the fifth evening Paul was being forced to suspect what he could hardly bear to believe. He noticed that whoever picked up the phone never bothered to call out to see if Ian was around, or needed to ask anyone else; mysteriously, they knew at once that he wasn't in. This time Paul pursued the matter, gently: "He seems to be out a great deal these days."

The voice at the other end hesitated.

"Er . . . yes."

"Is he away?"

"I think he may be in Edinburgh. Yes, I believe he's gone through to see his parents." There was a brief intake of breath; the owner of the voice had evidently realised his blunder.

"OK," Paul said quietly. "I'll try again sometime."

He was beginning to be tempted to hate Ian. Waves of anger would pass through him: was this the heterosexual way of dealing with an ex-affair? Was this their ceaselessly-trumpeted moral superiority to homosexuals? A gay man, he believed, would have let the affair turn into friendship – and besides, hadn't he and Ian been friends before they ever slept together? Was this any way to treat a friend?

Yet at other times he could feel no anger, only sadness. He couldn't forget the tenderness for Ian which had swept through him the evening after they returned from Edinburgh; the image of Ian asleep in the lamplight remained with him, partly a tormenting reminder of what he had lost, partly a continuing check on his rage. He had loved Ian then, and he loved him now; that was all there was to it.

One lunchtime, in a remainder bookshop, he found a book of photographs of Glasgow by night. It would make a perfect leaving present for Ian: substantial, but not expensive. He couldn't believe Ian could go on snubbing him for another three months. Apart from all else they were very likely to meet by chance, and even if they didn't, in the New Year he would go round to Ian's flat on some excuse, or to his studio, and catch him in. He was determined they weren't going to part like this, quarrelling because Ian wanted them to.

In the week before Christmas, on the Tuesday evening, he

tried ringing Ian's number yet again.

This time the answer was both more self-confident and more devastating: "I'm afraid he doesn't live here any more. He's moved out."

"Moved out?"

"Yes, he's gone to America."

Paul felt his heart literally stop and a fraction of a second later start again.

"America? You mean, for Christmas?"

"No, for good. He's gone back to live there. His wife lives there."

Paul struggled to speak: "When? When did he go?"

"He moved out on Sunday. Hang on a second." The person on the phone had a quick, muffled conversation with someone else, and then came back to the receiver: "We think he went to his parents for a few days. Maybe you could try there."

"Right, thanks," Paul said, and put the phone down. A second later he was diving towards a chest in the corner of the room; he flung it open and hunted out old diaries. In the back of his 1988 diary he found Ian's parents' address and phone number. His hand was shaking as he dialled again.

A woman answered: "Hallo?"

"Hi – I wonder if you can help me – I'm trying to get in touch with Ian, and I just wondered if you knew where he is?"

The woman laughed: "I certainly do – he's right here." She called out: "Ian! It's for you."

There was a pause of several seconds, and then Paul heard the so-familiar voice: "Hi?"

"Ian – it's Paul."

"Oh. Hi."

What to say?

"Your flatmates told me where you were. I hear you're leaving for America?"

"That's right."

"For good?"

"Yes."

"When?"

"On Thursday."

"Thursday?"

"Yes."

"That's the day after tomorrow?"

"Yes. The day after Wednesday."

"But . . . I thought you were staying on for your exhibition?"

"No."

"Well, what have you done about it?"

"I pulled out of it weeks ago."

It would have been impossible for his tone to be more hostile. He was plainly wild that Paul had stalked him down.

"Well, what are you going to do in America?"

"Don't know. Find a job, I hope."

"Aren't you going to go on painting?"

"I might. I suppose so."

The conversation limped on, agonisingly. The man who had once talked so fluently and vividly to Paul would now answer him only in monosyllables, and his tone darkened still further when Paul asked if they could meet the following day: "Absolutely not. It's a family day – saying goodbye to grandparents, all that."

"Can't you fit in a quick drink somewhere?"

"No."

"Well, how about tonight?"

"No. I'm busy all evening."

"So I won't be able to see you again?". Paul realised he was talking like an idiot.

"No."

"Well . . . Have you got your address in New York? Can you give me that?"

For some reason this seemed to ease Ian's fury; his voice became normal again as he dictated a combination of apartment, block, and street numbers: "That's going to be my address for the next few years. I hope!"

"Well," Paul said. "Well, I hope everything goes alright for you."

"Thanks."

Paul was numbed: he had no idea how to end the conversation.

"I have to go," Ian said. "I've a lot to do."

"Right. Well – see you some time when you're back?"

"Very likely."

"OK. Well – 'bye, then."

"'Bye."

And they hung up. As Paul put the phone down he doubted if he would ever see Ian again, or hear his voice.

He drank a huge tumbler of whisky, poured another, and rang Alex. They spoke for nearly an hour; Paul was still drinking and soon knew he was virtually incoherent: "The bastard!" he raged. "The fucking bastard! You've no idea how he fucking talked to me."

Alex sounded hardly less shocked than himself, but was calmer: "You know," he said, "no-one rejects someone like that unless they meant a lot to them in the first place."

"Eh?"

"He's obviously rejecting something in himself – his gayness. The whole gay side of him."

"Well, that's fucking obvious."

"Yes, but you must . . . You must mean more to him than just that."

"What are you saying? That he was in love with me?"

It was several seconds before Alex answered.

"Is that impossible?"

The idea had never once occurred to Paul. He was too tipsy to judge whether he believed it or not; but merely as a possibility it calmed him, and after he had finished talking to Alex he looked out the book he had bought as a present for Ian. In a drawer he found the photographs they had taken of each other on their day out in Edinburgh. He chose one which showed the Castle as background, and in the foreground Ian grinning with that air of a delighted schoolboy he had had when Paul looked up to see him in the Carnarvon. He pasted it on to the book's fly-leaf, and then wondered how to inscribe the book. On his shelves he found a Gaelic phrase-book; after a short hunt he identified something suitable, and wrote it above the photo: *Leis gach deagh dhurachd*. 'With every good wish'. It sounded less banal in the Gaelic. Then, drunk, he went to bed.

But when he woke up the following morning he was at once possessed by a rage which stayed with him while he ate and shaved and walked to work. It was like a thing in itself, alive apart from the rest of him; it refused to permit its existence to be forgotten for one instant; he believed that he had literally never been so angry in his life.

When he arrived at the office his secretary looked up, and immediately seemed startled.

"Are you alright?"

The question sobered Paul slightly. He realised he had let the state of his emotions become too apparent in his features: "No," he said simply. He added: "I'll explain later. Listen, can you get me the phone number for that firm of bike couriers we use?"

His secretary found it: "Shall I ring them?"

"No, I will. It's a personal matter."

Once he was inside his own office he called them: "Could you courier a parcel for me from the West End to East Kilbride?"

They could. They would be at the office within fifteen minutes.

Paul took the book he had bought for Ian out of his briefcase and put it in a jiffy-bag. Then he seized a plain sheet of paper and scribbled the date. He couldn't bring himself to write 'Dear Ian', so without any preliminary he started:

> I intended to give you the enclosed as a leaving present when we met for a farewell drink – since that fell through, you might as well have it anyway.

This sounded so rude he decided to hurriedly qualify it with a joke:

> The saving in the costs of the booze will pay for the courier! If he turns up in leather, my day will be made.

He paused. What now? There wasn't time to draft

anything elaborate; he could only go on spontaneously:

> I'm sorry you've chosen to leave under such a cloud of unfriendliness – *very* sorry. I don't see any need for it and maybe, in retrospect, neither will you. It seems a sad end to some very happy times. We had some great laughs together! I'd like to have ended on a laugh, too.

He sat and looked at the last sentence; was it grammatical? But now he needed an ending. Suddenly a sentence of such delicious bitchiness came to him he wrote it down before he could have doubts about it:

> Hoping you get on better in America second time round.
>
> Paul

He folded the letter and put it in the bag. Five minutes later the courier arrived – not in leather, but in thick winter gear.

The courier didn't know East Kilbride, a few miles outside Glasgow, and they had to pore together over his map before they located Ian's address. After he had left the office Paul went to the window and looked down at him in the street; he was still studying the map, spread out over the bike's pillion.

As last he folded it up and got on to the bike. It revved loudly; he turned and went slowly to the bottom of the street, stopped, and then roared off, along Woodlands Road and out of Paul's sight.

Paul turned back into his office. He saw the files piled on the side of his desk, the correspondence waiting for his attention. He sighed deeply; to some extent with relief that the courier, biking through the streets of Glasgow, was carrying to Ian his bitterness and his rage.

In the evening he worked on his Dutch, which he was studying again in preparation for his move to Amsterdam. The intellectual effort of struggling with an awkward grammar and strange vocabulary helped to distract him from his thoughts, and at one point it even amused him: *Heb je veel boeken gelezen?*, the cassette asked. Have you read many books? "Of course I have," Paul growled. "I'm a fucking publisher."

Afterwards he sat reading and slowly drinking whisky. For a long time he didn't listen to any music because he couldn't think of anything which would fit his mood. But late on, after midnight, he hunted out another of the photographs he had taken in Edinburgh and propped it on the mantelpiece. It was a close-up of Ian; in it he was gazing at the camera with a slight frown of attention. Paul knew that expression well: it was how he had looked whenever Paul was expounding his side in one of their long, intricate pub discussions.

He went to his stereo and selected the only music he could think of as even half-appropriate; a few moments later the dark opening chords of *Don Giovanni* struck out from his speakers. He returned to his chair and sat gazing at the photo on the mantelpiece. Well, he thought, I don't know which of us comes out of this looking the worse. You've shown yourself to be a total bastard, and I've been shown up to be a total fool. Maybe, Ian, we're quits.

But as soon as the thought had passed he was ashamed of it. Alex's voice recurred to him: "There's no point in being bitter, Paul". True enough. And he remembered something else Alex had said: was it possible that Ian had been in love with him? Was that really the explanation of why, in these last weeks of his time in Scotland, Ian had rejected him so unrelentingly? It seemed very improbable; but as Paul drank from his whisky he pondered the idea.

Suddenly he smiled. Did it, in the end, matter? If one of them was a bastard and the other a fool – who would want a world without bastards and fools? Who would want to lead a sensible life surrounded by the good and the just? He turned his eyes to Ian's photo: maybe you're a shit, he addressed him mentally, but you're a shit who was fun to know. And loving you reminded me of what I live for. He smiled again and raised his glass. "Here's looking at you, kid", he said softly.

Notes on Scottish Expressions and Institutions

Aberdeen	In effect the capital of the northeastern region of Scotland, which has its own very distinctive dialect and accent, and a much more conservative culture than central Scotland.
Aye	(As an adverb): always
BB	Boys Brigade; a youth organisation similar to the Scouts.
Bide	Stay
Book of Kells	Ninth-century manuscript of the Gospels, possibly begun on the island of Iona in Scotland and certainly belonging to the period when Ireland and western Scotland were one flourishing Celtic civilisation. Beyond question the greatest of the Celtic illuminated manuscripts, it can now be seen in the Library of Trinity College, Dublin.
Brae	Hill or slope
Burgh	The Scots spelling of 'borough'; pronounced the same way. A Royal Burgh was a burgh which had received its charter from the Crown; in the Middle Ages they had exclusive rights to trade overseas. Royal Burghs were abolished with local government re-organisation in the early 1970s.
Burn	Stream
Carse	An alluvial plain, used mainly for arable farming.

Celtic Glasgow football club founded in 1888 by the Irish Catholic community, and still predominantly, but not exclusively, supported by Catholics. Once one of the greatest clubs in Europe (v. Stein, Jock) but now in serious decline. (The name of the football club, unlike the normal adjective, is pronounced with a soft 'c'.)

Chiel Man. North-eastern usage.

Dookin Ducking or bobbing for apples (at Halloween)

Draw the belt Of a schoolteacher: to be able to use the belt with particular effectiveness. Invariably used approvingly. Now obsolete. (V. Scottish education system.)

Dreich Roughly: dreary, damp, depressing. Difficult to translate but in the Scottish climate easy to experience.

Eighty Short for 'eighty-shilling'; a type of Scottish beer very similar to English bitter. The name refers to the former excise value of the beer, which depended on its alcoholic strength – therefore 'seventy-shilling' is weaker than eighty, and 'ninety-shilling' would flatten Superman.

England The largest nation of the United Kingdom, lying south of Scotland (q.v.) and east of Wales. *England is not the same entity as Britain.*

Fenian Originally a term for nineteenth-century Irish nationalists, now West of Scotland slang for a Catholic or a Celtic supporter.

Foulis Press The Glasgow University Press 1741-75, run by the Foulis brothers, Robert and Andrew. Their editions are still highly prized for a clarity of printing, particularly of the Greek classics, which they pioneered. (With acknowledgements to RDI.)

Gaelic The ancient Celtic language of Scotland, now spoken by only a small minority of people. Not to be confused with Scots, the close cognate of English used for example by Burns.

Gait In Scots, a place where you gang, or go – ie, a street.

Glasgow Fair The traditional annual Glasgow holiday in July, founded in the twelfth century. Now usually takes the form of a long weekend, like an English Bank Holiday, but still to some extent a two-week trades holiday.

Gowk Fool

Gurly Angry, rough

Harled Pebble-dashed

Jacobite A supporter of the exiled Stuart King James VIII and III, q.v.

James VIII King of Scots; James III of England. Rightful King of Britain 1701-1766, but barred from his throne by the usurpation of the unspeakable Hanoverians, progenitors of the Mountbatten- Windsors.

Ken Know

Knowe Knoll

Licks Strokes of the belt (v. Scottish education system). North-eastern usage.

Loun Boy. Very much a north-eastern word. (Pronounced 'loon' and more often spelt that way, but for obvious reasons I prefer the alternative spelling. Aberdonians form a diminutive by adding *-ie* at the end of a word (cf. the Dutch *-je*), so the Aberdonian for a small boy is 'loonie'.)

Menteith This is a real and ancient name, of Pictish origin. 'Carse of Menteith', however, is an invented place-name, but not Lake of Menteith, which is famous for being the only lake in Scotland – all other inland waters are of course lochs.

Mince Rubbish. Glasgow slang.

Muirland Moorland

Owre Too, as in 'too late', etc.

Rangers Glasgow football club founded in 1873 and until 1989 rigidly non-Catholic. Currently the unchallenged leading club in Scotland.

Scotland Some key aspects of this book will be incomprehensible if the reader does not understand that the great majority of Scots feel they are leaving their home country as soon as they cross the Border into England. Since 1707 Scotland and England have been united as Great Britain, but Scotland retains entrenched national rights within the Union and very considerable distinguishing characteristics, notably a separate legal system, education system (q.v.), politics, banks, paper money, dialects, accents, literature, styles of architecture, forms of popular music, etc, etc, etc.

Scottish education system

The Scottish education system differs radically from the English system. For the first seven years of education Scottish school-children attend primary school, where the classes are numbered Primary One, Primary Two, etc. They then spend a maximum of six years at secondary school, where the classes are numbered First Year, Second Year, etc. There is no division into 'Lower' and 'Upper' Sixth. It is important to note that because Scottish children go up to secondary school a year later than their English counterparts, Paul's Third Year at Eassord Academy equates to the English Fourth Form. The Scottish school year begins in mid-August and runs till the end of the following June.

The qualifying certificate for university entrance, Highers, is taken at the end of Fifth Year, and Scottish pupils can therefore leave school for university a year earlier than pupils in England, as Paul chooses to do in this novel. At the end of two years a Scottish university course divides: one further year is required to obtain an Ordinary degree, but a further two for an Honours degree. Most students therefore spend four years as undergraduates.

Almost all Scottish state schools have always been what in England is called 'co-educational'. Until the abolition of the 11-

plus in the early 1970s secondary schools were divided into 'senior secondaries', roughly the equivalent of English grammar schools, and 'junior secondaries', the equivalent of English secondary moderns.

Until the early 1980s corporal punishment was used far more regularly in Scotland than in England. Paul is quite exceptional in being belted at his secondary school only three times in three years; many boys at that period were belted this often in a term. The instrument employed was a leather belt approximately 50 cm long and half a centimetre thick, divided at the 'business' end into two tails (occasionally three). It was almost invariably applied to the hands. Having used corporal punishment to an obscene excess Scotland then abolished it altogether, before it was abolished in England – a remarkable illustration of the tendency of the Scots to inhabit extremes and disdain the *via media* of the English.

Scottish nationalist A supporter of the restoration of Scottish independence.

Scottish Regalia The ancient Crown, Sceptre, and Sword of State of the Scottish kingdom.

Stein, Jock Manager of Celtic FC 1965-78. The 1965 Cup Final which Paul hears on the radio in 'A Springtime of Beginnings' was the start of Celtic's glory years, when Stein led them to a wealth of honours, including the European Cup and nine League titles in a row.

Sunset Song The first part of Lewis Grassic Gibbon's *A Scots Quair*, set in the north east of Scotland in the years just before and during the First World War. Beyond question the greatest Scottish novel of the century.

Stooshie Argument, fight

Tallies A café or shop run by Italians. It is important to note that, unlike 'Paki', this word had no offensive connotations.

Wean (Pronounced 'wain'): child. West of Scotland usage. (Short for 'wee one'.)

Also available from Millivres Books

Summer Set

David Evans

When pop singer Ludo Morgan's elderly bulldog pursues animal portraitist Victor Burke - wearing womens' underwear beneath his leathers - to late night Hampstead Heath a whole sequence of events is set in train. Rescued by the scantily-clad and utterly delicious Nick Longingly, only son of his closest friend Kitty Llewellyn, Victor finds himself caught up in a web of emotional and physical intrigue which can only be resolved when the entire cast of this enormously diverting novel abandon London and head off for a weekend in Somerset.

ISBN 1 873741 02 2 £7.50

'Immensely entertaining . . .' Patrick Gale, *Gay Times*

Also available from Millivres Books

On the Edge

Sebastian Beaumont

In this auspicious debut novel set in the north of England, nineteen year old Peter Ellis is on the edge of discovery both about the artist father he never knew and whom his mother refuses to discuss and about the direction of his own life. Although he has heterosexual relationships with the teenaged Anna and the somewhat perverse art student Coll, it is with his life-long friend Martin, himself a painter of promise, that Peter seems happiest. On the Edge combines elements of a thriller - the mystery surrounding the life and sudden death of Peter's father - and passionate ambisextrous romance and provides an immensely readable narrative about late adolescence, sexuality and creativity.

ISBN 1 873741 00 6 £6.99

'Mr Beaumont writes with assurance and perception . . .'
Tom Wakefield *Gay Times*

Also available from Millivres Books

Heroes Are Hard to Find

Sebastian Beaumont

When his long-time lover returns to Greece to set up a new life for them both, Rick has to adjust to being on his own for the six months of their separation. He lives in Brighton and works as a model, meeting new friends, including the enigmatic Gary and the extraordinary Max, a hedonistic quadriplegic. Rick seems to be surviving the separation until he meets Oliver – a strangely charismatic young man with uninterpretable motives - and, in spite of a growing sense of community, he finds himself in a turmoil.

Heroes Are Hard to Find is a compelling, sometimes comic, sometimes unbearably moving novel about sexual infatuation, infidelity and deceit. It is also about disability, death and the joy of living.

ISBN 1 873741 08 1 £7.50

'I cheered, felt proud and cried aloud . . . I simply cannot recommend this book enough . . . A must . . .' *All Points North*

Millivres Books can be ordered from any bookshop in the UK and from specialised bookshops overseas. If you prefer to order by mail, please send full retail price plus 80p (UK) or £2.00 (overseas) per title for postage and packing to:
Dept MBks
Millivres Ltd
Ground Floor
Worldwide House
116-134 Bayham Street
London NW1 0BA

A comprehensive catalogue is available on request.